The Wild Fields

The Wild Fields

A Fight for the Soul of Ukraine

Paul D. LeFavor

"When bad men combine, the good must associate; else they will fall, one by one, an unpitied sacrifice in a contemptible struggle."
– Edmund Burke

Contents

Testament – Taras Shevchenko

When I die, then make my grave
High on an ancient mound,
In my own beloved Ukraine,
In steppeland without bound:
Whence one may see wide-skirted
wheatland,
Dnipro's steep-cliffed shore,
There whence one may hear the blustering
River wildly roar.

Till from Ukraine to the blue sea
It bears in fierce endeavour
The blood of foemen — then I'll leave
Wheatland and hills forever:
Leave all behind, soar up until
Before the throne of God
I'll make my prayer.
For till that hour
I shall know naught of God.

Make my grave there — and arise,
Sundering your chains,
Bless your freedom with the blood
Of foemen's evil veins!
Then in that great family,
A family new and free,
Do not forget, with good intent
Speak quietly of me.

Map of the Donbas

Map of Zolote

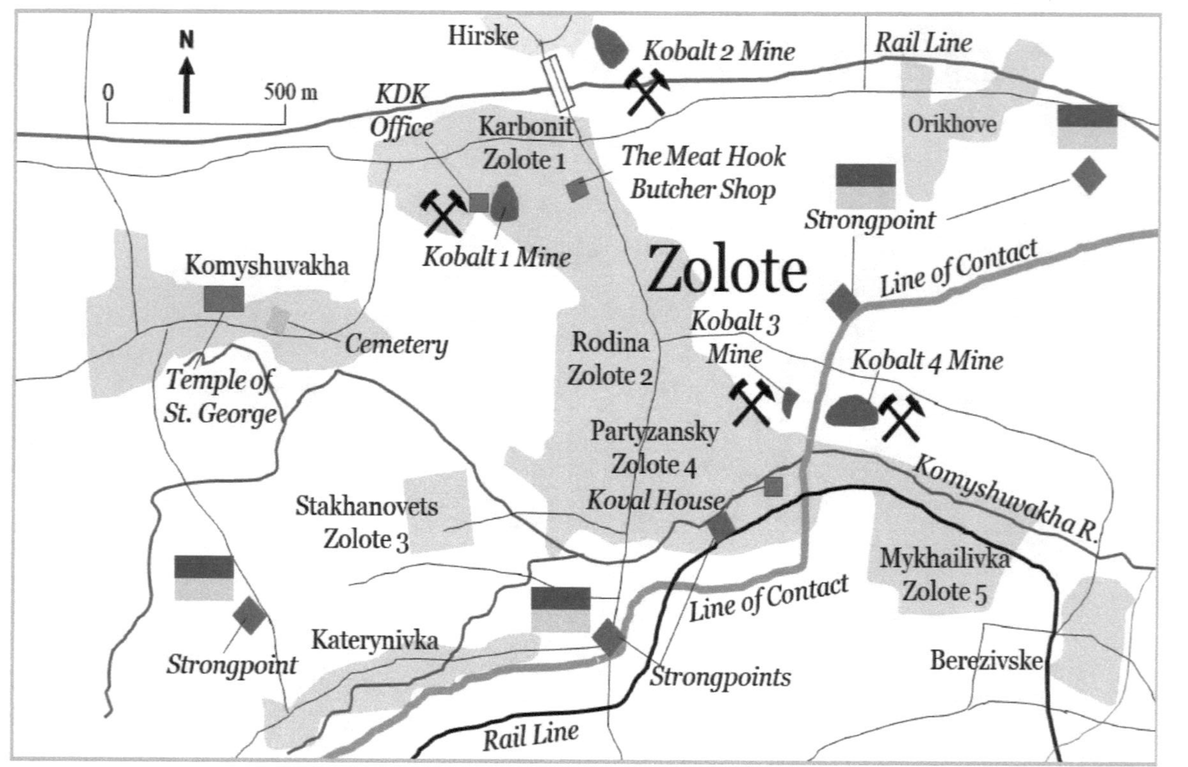

*To my mother, Rosemary LeFavor,
a woman of great worth, whose
children rise up to call her blessed!*

The Funeral

The life he lived, which appeared to be a search for meaning, or a story seeking a conclusion, was essentially that of a man in search of himself; and depending on the day, it could be either a drama or a tragedy. The azure tiles on the roof of the Temple of St. George glistened brightly. The glint of the cross on its magnificent golden-domed tower could be seen for miles. The afternoon was perfectly clear. A warm July breeze carried choral melodies out of its windows and into the surrounding fields. Such music was a welcomed guest to the Donbas coal-mining town of Zolote. It was now the fifth year of the war, and the town, whose name means 'golden,' straddled the so-called 'gray zone' of war-ravaged Eastern Ukraine.

Inside the orthodox sanctuary, a festival of light and life was celebrated. Employing all the elements that make up the divine liturgy: the cross, the chalice, icons, candles, hymns of praise, and the blaze of color in the priests' vestments, all gave credence to the power of something 'otherworldly.' Incense from the priest's thurible slowly waft upward, filling the sacred enclosure with a sweet, perfumed scent. Adding to the ambiance, Kievan chants sounded forth ancient words of eternal significance and earthly hope.

With all its celestial brilliance, the atmosphere within the church seemed to become ethereal, like that of heaven itself. One might be enraptured with all the glories of that undiscovered country had it not been for the cold deadness of the casket lying at the base of the altar. The shiny black coffer contained the mortal remains of Taras Kolisnychenko, found dead in a nearby field two days prior.

Atop the altar, flanked by two decorative candles and an ornate casket spray of flowers, was a single framed photograph of the young man. In it, he was seen standing in front of the gold-domed monastery of St. Michael's in Kyiv. The bright, smiling-faced lad in the photograph contrasted starkly with the gray-toned waxen visage in the open casket. His body was washed and clothed in white, signifying that it now belonged to another world. The look on his face was tragic, befitting the nature of his death. Wrapped around his waist was a black belt, and on his forehead, in a solemn prayer for grace, was a cloth with the words "Holy God, Holy Mighty, Holy Immortal, have mercy on us."

Seated toward the back of the sanctuary, offering him a commanding view, sat a man taking in the solemnity of the funeral mass. In his early fifties, he wore his graying hair short-cropped, and sported a longer variety goatee that was accentuated by two broad streaks of gray. Feeling hot and irritable, he gripped the arm of the wooden pew and shifted his weight, emitting a faint crack from his lower torso.

The man fixed his gaze on the young man in the casket as if listening to him speak. They exchanged a glance. The man took in a long, deep breath, detecting a coalescence of scents: the comforting fragrance of incense, the delicate piquancy of flowers, a redolence of the many candles emitting the trace of baked cinnamon, under all of which he traced a faintly detectable evocative whiff of formaldehyde. The man swallowed as if to force back some overwhelming emotion. The entire mood of the funeral was suffocating him. He felt a sudden tightness in his chest. Gripped by an unnamed fear, he did his best not to panic, shuddering as if he had seen a phantom. His heart palpitated. Growing dizzy, he looked away. Looking around at the assembled congregation, he started to number who was there, but then lost count somewhere after a hundred.

Glancing back at the young man, he discovered he couldn't look at the boy's face so much as a few seconds before re-experiencing the same phenomenon as before.

"Why would anyone murder him?" whispered the man to another.

"He wasn't a soldier; he was a coal miner, barely eighteen."

"It's not the first time nor the last that we'll see a young man in a casket. Isn't that so, Pavel?"

"Yeah, but when a miner dies, it's normally by a cave in, toxic fumes, or any other myriad of causes in the subterranean world. The official police report ruled mortar fire. No way," said Pavel, shaking his head.

"What's so hard to believe? The cease-fire is broken nearly a hundred times every week. Errant bullets and stray mortar rounds are a daily occurrence. People just go about their lives as best they can. Even the schools and shops stay open," said Stepan.

Pavel looked at his friend, "But twenty-one people killed from casual mortars and errant bullets in six months is a bit excessive, even for a town in the gray zone! Besides, no one expected this damn war to last so long!"

"My dear friend, if sporadic gunfire is so much a part of our daily lives, why would anyone be surprised when it touches us?" replied Stepan.

"All the same, the report is bogus. I just know it... and I hate funerals," said Pavel.

"Why is that?" asked Stepan.

"We are told funerals are for the living to celebrate the life of the dead. Instead, all the living do is think about death. I don't need to attend a funeral to do that. I swear this is my last funeral... ever."

Pavel sat back and looked up at the ceiling. It was stifling hot in the sanctuary, even with the doors and windows open. Pavel leaned over to his friend. "Besides, he's the third one this month! But not from mining, mind you."

"You suspect foul play?" wondered Stepan.

"The answer's clear to any fool."

"Only, we live in a war zone. And in war, the innocent always suffer. Hence, only the dead see the end of war," said Stepan.

"No philosophizing. Not now. I admire your stoicism, I really do. I like seeing it work for you. The trouble is, I just can't make it work for myself. I admire the whole cognitive system of cardinal virtues, the path of eudaimonia, ataraxic tranquility and the like."

Stepan grinned as Pavel traced out the fundamentals of the ancient philosophical system.

"I suppose you're thinking, what's happened to this poor lad was merely waiting from the beginning of time to happen?"

"That's true," said Stepan, "there's no escape when God decides your days are numbered."

"Do you say that from inner peace, or your resignation to fate?" questioned Pavel.

"My dear friend, the willing are led by fate, the reluctant are dragged."

Pavel smiled. Looking around at the veritable army of mosaic paintings along the walls, and the iconostasion separating the nave from the sanctuary, he sensed the host of heaven standing sentinel over the altar. He began counting the number of candles, but soon lost count.

"Why can't the beauty and peace we have in here go out there," wondered Pavel.

Pavel's wife, Yelizaveta, leaned over. "Darling please, it's a funeral."

Pavel nodded in assent. Then looking back at the young man's face, he thought, "All your love, all your hate, has long since vanished. Your hopes and dreams all dashed to oblivion in one fell swoop. They say death has a dignity all its own, but where's the dignity in your death?"

He looked again at the boy's face, staring as long as he dared. Then overcome again with intense dread, he glanced away. Finding it increasingly difficult to sit in such close proximity to the dead, he leaned to one side, then another, unable to get comfortable. It was becoming increasingly hot. He could feel his sweat against his back as he fidgeted in the pew.

It was his fifth funeral this year. He had sat through many others before. What was perplexing him so? He settled himself again in the pew. Then, hearing the bawling of a baby, he began to feel fidgety again, as the crying grew louder. His wife seemed not to notice. No one seemed to notice. What bothered him most was that the crying didn't seem to bother anyone.

Pavel mused, thinking of all the times he'd sat in the church, taking in this same view. The liturgy of the mass continued with a prayerful dialogue, passing by way of chants between the priests and the people. Then the time came for the priest to give a short homily. As Father Malashenko made his way to the cloth-draped lectern, Pavel breathed a sigh of relief, glancing up at the radiant beams of light illuminating the heavenly paintings on the ceiling above.

Father Volodymyr Malashenko came to Zolote in the spring of 2015. His predecessor, Father Honchar, abandoned the church in the wake of the violence and chaos that came with the war. One story had it that Father Honchar left in haste with as many icons, crosses, and candles as he could carry. However, after Father Malashenko arrived, and the townspeople saw his diligent care for them, there ended up being more than enough holy things, as the people donated icons and the like; some of which had been hidden since the time of the Soviets.

With each hand clamping down on the podium, Father Malashenko looked out at the congregation, and in a simple but solemn tone, began:

"There's always two sides to every story. One side says Kyiv started the war when they told us we had to learn to speak Ukrainian. The other says the Kremlin just wants to reclaim the glory days of Stalin. Now, all the philosophy in the world's collective coffers can't seem to untie this Gordian knot of a problem that we find ourselves in. Our home is in a warzone. Armored columns rattle down our streets. Homes have been raked with machinegun fire, and after five years of killing, more than thirteen thousand of our countrymen have died. Yet, our problem is not political; it's spiritual. Our ancient and deadly foe has sown his evil seed amongst us. As we look at our problems, can we see it? It's our spiritual problems that have brought about this great carnage that we now experience."

He sighed deeply. "Friends, consider the words of St. Paul, who in the sixth chapter of his epistle to the Ephesians writes: 'For we wrestle not against flesh and blood, but against principalities, against powers, against the rulers of the darkness of this age, against spiritual hosts of wickedness in the heavenly places.' In other words, our enemies are not flesh and blood, but rather supernatural evil. May the Lord enable us to see this truth before it's too late, before we all kill each other. May the grace and peace of Christ lead us to resolve our differences and bring an end to this war. Now, my friends, I know there are many of you here who are suffering. Let me offer you the Bible's counsel. There are two ways to respond: the first way curses God because of suffering, and the second praises God in spite of it. We mustn't judge God's love based on the bad that comes along. We all face things that we don't like. But facing them with the hope that only God can give us, makes all the difference. Now, this young man had a bright and promising future, but his light was snuffed out by the ravages of this war. Let it be said then, dear friends, that the eyes of the Lord are in everyplace beholding the good, as well as the evil. Be assured, no evil deed will go unpunished. Nothing will be swept under the rug of the universe. So, take heart my friends. The Judge of all the earth will right the wrong. What a man sows, he reaps.

Lastly, let it be said that death separates all other relations, but the soul's union with Christ is not dissolved in the grave," he said, pointing his hand over to the casket.

"Though Taras's body will be laid in the grave, one day Christ will return, and the trumpet will sound, and this mortal body will put on immortality, and this decomposing, decaying body will become imperishable."

He then slowly gave the sign of the cross and chanted the words, "In the name of the Father, and the Son, and the Holy Ghost. Amen."

Making his way to the door, he gave the benediction, then led those bearing the casket outside to the graveside. Following the traditional manner, one man took the lead, carrying the cross. In his footsteps was Father Malashenko with the thurible, leading the people in the singing of the Trisagion, "Holy God, Holy Strong, Holy Immortal, have mercy on us."

As the church bells sounded forth solemn tones, some two hundred mourners cued in the procession. In the modern style, not many wore black. Instead, due to the stifling heat, most were clad in thinner clothing; some even wore shorts. The procession wound its way down the path to the graveside, which was a mere five hundred meters from the churchyard. As Pavel and his family joined them, he recognized one of his friends, Yakiv, a coal miner. He had been selected to be one of the pallbearers. They each exchanged a solemn nod.

"Better him than me," thought Pavel. For him, taking part in what he felt was a corporate gesture of despair, became an arduous chore. All he could think about was getting back home to enjoy what was left of his Sunday. Though his conscience bothered him for such a thought, he repeatedly glanced at his watch, nonetheless.

The road flowed gently down the side of the hill to the graveyard, which was neatly hedged with trees. To the south, could be seen the river valley and beyond that the town of Zolote. The old carved gates of the graveyard hung open in welcome as the procession reached its terminus.

Then the pallbearers gently, and in the most dignified manner possible, lowered the casket, readying it for its descent into the black soil. Except for the wind, all movement then ceased. The scent of the freshly turned earth hung in the air. Standing around at attention, the neat rows of gravestones welcomed their new neighbor. Opposite this stone garden, an army of sunflowers, with their sunbaked brilliant petals saluted the new arrival.

The dead boy's mother then approached the casket. She was trembling and held by a man of the family. Tears welled in her eyes, then streamed down her cheeks. With flowers in her hand, she wiped her tears and pressed her cheek to the boy's face. She held herself there for a long moment, muttering softly. This scene repeated itself until all the family said their last farewell. Then the rest of the bereaved paid their final respects. Finally, the casket was closed and the mother laid an assortment of flowers on the casket: a most beautiful bushel of yellow roses and blue iris.

Father Malashenko then read the sacred text out of the Book of Job, saying, "For I know that my Redeemer lives, and He shall stand at last on the earth; and after my skin is destroyed, this I know, that in my flesh I shall see God, whom I shall see for myself, and my eyes shall behold, and not another."

He then led everyone in the four hymns, which reached its zenith with the words, "O only pure and spotless holy Virgin, intercede for the salvation of the soul of your servant."

Slowly giving the sign of the cross, he began to chant once again the Trisagion, saying, "Holy God, Holy Strong, Holy Immortal, have mercy on us."

Pouring oil on the casket, the priest made the sign of the cross and said, "Sprinkle me with hyssop, and I shall be pure; cleanse me, and I shall be whiter than snow."

In an instant, the greedy soil absorbed all traces of the oil. Then, four men with cloth ropes slowly lowered the casket into the black earth. The casket's slow descent was accompanied by the loud wails and cries from family and friends. Leaning forward with morbid curiosity, Pavel strained to take in a final glimpse. The wails and moans of the family continued as the casket slowly and steadily descended.

After it made its full descent, Father Malashenko cast sand on the grave and said, "You are dust and to dust you shall return."

"It seems our hopes for this war to be finally over are being buried along with this young man," thought Pavel.

As he heard the ropes whip back to the surface, the last sound the grave made was a gentle rattling of dirt against the coffin.

"Maybe that's it," thought Pavel, "we'll all just end up killing each other, but then who would mourn and bury us?"

2

Vasyli's Tale

Only a handful of buildings like these remained in Zolote; at least those left somewhat unmolested by the hands of war. It was a five-story Soviet-era block apartment complex. Known as Khrushchev slums, clusters of these apartments could be found from the Black Sea to the Urals. However ubiquitous, none could be found in Zolote in such fair condition.

Most of the town's buildings that lay a kilometer or two from the so-called 'line of contact' were shell pocked from legions of machinegun, rocket, and mortar fire exchanges. Especially scarred were the buildings facing the trenches. With nearly every window blown out, these bore the wounds of a thousand skirmishes. Regarding the grounds in and around such buildings, one could scarcely walk without falling into an artillery crater.

Just on the outskirts of Partyzansky, the concrete-paneled brick apartment was home to Pavel Koval and his family. Partyzansky, also known as Zolote 4, was one of five villages that merged to create the town of Zolote. The others, Kobalt, Rodina, Stakhanovets, and Mykhailivka, constitute Zolote 1, 2, 3, and 5 respectively.

The apartment was not far from the Koval family's old home in Zolote 5, which was now part of the self-proclaimed Luhansk People's Republic. Though their new home was less spacious, it nonetheless had power and water, while many other buildings did not have such a luxury. Moreover, it offered a bird's eye view of the trench line.

The Kovals had lived in Zolote for three generations. Pavel's grandparents, Mykola and Anna Koval, moved to the coal-mining town in the 1950s under Khrushchev. Totting along their infant son Vasyli, the couple left Mariupol in search of a better life. Mykola found work in the mines. In those days, coalmining was in its hay day. Every miner sought to be the next Alexey Stakhanov, who once famously dug one hundred two tons of coal in a single six-hour shift.

Mining coal placed Zolote on the map, yet the subterranean industry had long held a central role in the history of Eastern Ukraine. In the 1870s, the Welshman John Hughes was invited to help develop the coal productivity of the Donbas, short for Donets Basin. The success of Hughes' enterprising labor led to the founding of the city of Donetsk, which was originally named Hughesovka in his honor. Then in 1924, it was renamed Stalino, after Stalin, and finally became Donetsk in 1961. Energized by the entrepreneurial spirit of Hughes, the Donbas soon developed into the principal iron-producing region. In fact, it became the largest in what was then the Russian Empire. In the 1900s, the Donbas became so productive that it accounted for some seventy percent of Russia's overall iron productivity.

Like his father, the young Vasyli took to the mines; his large frame was well suited to the work. Without complaint, he'd spend nearly half the day, Monday through Saturday, below the earth's surface. One day in the summer of 1963, he met Nina. They fell in love and married the following year. While he loved Nina, Vasyli loathed the hard work in the mines. He could feel it killing him.

As he told her on one occasion, "In mining, there are simply too many ways to die: being buried alive under falling coal, poisoned by underground fumes, or a hundred other ways to get maimed. And if you survive, you live the rest of your days literally fighting for breath. This was the fate of my father, Mykola Koval. One day, he was taken up for dead. He had long suffered from miner's asthma from the many years of inhaling coal dust. And so, like many other miners, he had literally dug his own grave."

After giving it much thought, Vasyli felt he had to get out before it claimed his life too.

It was the entrepreneurial spirit of the Kovals that led Vasyli to seek out a more congenial occupation. By chance, he was offered an apprenticeship in a butcher shop. Though he knew virtually nothing about the work of being a butcher, a lot can be said for a great work ethic. The man took him on, and Vasyli's fortune turned for the best.

Providence smiled on Vasyli again when Pavel was born; then three years later, Laryssa. Vasyli and Nina then went on to live a full life together. Vasyli watched Nina's beautiful brown hair mature to a smoky gray, then a winter white. When she died in 2015, Vasyli moved in with his son Pavel and his family. It was a convenient yet commendable arrangement.

Два

It was Sunday evening. The Kovals had returned from the funeral mass and spent several hours preparing their apartment for guests. Pavel and Vasyli tidied up the living room, while Yelizaveta prepared a feast. As was customary, Pavel had invited some of his friends to dinner. The first to arrive was Anton Chornyi. Always punctual, Anton was never one to miss a meal. He was one of Pavel's comrades from the Soviet-Afghan War. The two had served in the Red Army together and battled the mujahideen[1] in the 1980s. He was one of the few veterans that Pavel kept in touch with.

---

[1] Muslims who fight on behalf of the Islamic faith.

Outside the apartment, Anton was met with the faint sound of music playing on the radio. He walked up the four flights of stairs, accompanied by the music of a Ukrainian love song, taking in the tantalizing aromas.

"Salo and liver stuffed varenyky?" queried Anton, breaking the apartment's threshold. He and Pavel exchanged a brotherly handshake.

"And borscht," added Yelizaveta, stepping out of the kitchen.

Even with the windows open, the piquant aromas filled every square inch of the cramped apartment. Pavel's wife, Yelizaveta, was a fine cook, knowing all the old recipes.

"Did you hear about Boryslav? Boryslav Popov?" asked Anton. "Do you remember him?"

"Yes. How could I forget? He was quite a comedian; he always kept our spirits up, especially in dark times. How is he?" asked Pavel.

"He died last week," said Anton. "I'm sorry to be the one telling you. I guess you could say, the war finally claimed him. He was always telling me how he couldn't seem to leave it behind. Sorry, I didn't mean to be so melancholy. I just thought you should know."

"Thank you," replied Pavel phlegmatically.

Pavel brought Anton to the living room, doing his best not to dwell on the troubling news. Then, he walked into the kitchen.

"Stepan can't make it tonight. We'll just need eight place settings," said Pavel.

"Well, that's understandable," said Yelizaveta. "I'm sure he got busy; maybe next time."

Fyodor, Anton's son, was next to arrive. He gave a greeting to Pavel's daughters, Savka and Tatyana, squeezed Anna's cheek, then found his way to the table. Last to arrive was Victor Nimchuk, a strong, handsome man in his early twenties who worked for the Kovals at their family butcher shop. By now, the tiny three-bedroom apartment was so cramped, that with all the cooking underway, it felt like a sauna.

"Welcome to our humble abode," said Pavel.

"The funny thing about these old apartments is, they're so difficult to tell apart from other buildings, that a man could stumble into a strange woman's apartment and insist it was his own!" said Pavel; everyone laughed. The table that comfortably sat six was covered with a setting for nine, as every inch of the tabletop was economized.

"I feel like we are sardines," smirked Tatyana.

"Father, would you say the blessing?" requested Pavel.

Vasyli prayed: "Father of all, we pray to you for the late young Taras, and for all those whom we love, but see no longer. Grant him eternal rest. Let Your perpetual light shine upon him. May his soul and the souls of all the departed, through the mercy of God, rest in peace... O Christ God, bless the food and drink of Thy servants, for Thou art holy, always, now and ever, and unto ages of ages. Amen."

"Amen," said everyone in unison.

"It's hard to remember such a good time," said Vasyli, as they all sat down to the feast that Yelizaveta had prepared.

"Yes," replied Tatyana, smiling to all their guests, "a fine meal can transport you to another world, and to happier times."

"Yes, indeed. Well said," exclaimed Vasyli.

Tatyana was a rare combination of beauty and innocence. As she walked around the table, she poured the wine as everyone took their seats. Receiving a playful wink from Victor, she winked back.

"You could say this is our little wake for the late young Taras. It's good we honor him," said Tatyana.

"It was just a ceremony. It doesn't mean anything. It's nothing more than an antiquated ritual created by the church," said Savka with callous indignity.

"The funeral? What do you mean, 'it doesn't mean anything'?" asked Tatyana.

"It's just an antiquated ritual."

"It was sacred and beautiful. Don't you believe in an afterlife? In heaven and hell?" snapped Tatyana.

"Girls!" said Yelizaveta nervously, in an attempt to quell what appeared to be another fight.

Anton dug into his food ravenously. "The food is simply spectacular!"

Savka shot a deathly stare at Tatyana.

"How are things at the mobile kitchen?" asked Anton.

"Very good, last Friday we fed over twenty," replied Yelizaveta.

"Anyone can get food? Bread? And other things?" he asked further.

"Yes, they also give out medicines," she said as she followed Tatyana, doling out servings of varenyky.

"You have such a good heart," said Anton.

"Just trying to do my part to ease the suffering."

"Tatyana, when will you go back to Odessa?" asked Victor.

"I'm not."

"Really?" asked Anton. "I thought you were pursuing a law degree?"

"Not anymore."

"May I ask why?" inquired Victor.

"The world has changed and so have I. Besides, I had to come help my family," she said, receiving a heartfelt smile from her mother.

"I thought Father Malashenko did a fine job today, didn't you Grandpa?" asked Yelizaveta.

"Indeed, he did. And he's right, there are always two sides to every story," said Vasyli.

"I thought it was a bit too political," interjected Fyodor.

"Really?" questioned Vasyli.

"I agree. Enough is politicized already. Why bring it into the church?" asked Savka.

"I thought his position was rather conciliatory," chimed in Vasyli, passing a bowl of food.

"Besides, regardless of one's position, you must admit, this war touches everyone. People with no interest in the Crimea or the Donbas have been caught up in the lunacy of this war. If you doubt this, consider those who perished in the downing of that Malaysian airliner."

In an attempt to cut the tension, Victor asked Pavel if it would be okay if he gave the first toast.

"Yes, it should be you. You were good friends," said Pavel.

Victor stood up, raising his glass, prompting everyone to raise theirs.

"Taras Kolisnychenko was a good man. He worked hard and never complained. He once had a dream that he shared with me. He wanted more than anything to live by the Black Sea and be a fisherman," he said as he laughed.

"To a good man with a heart of gold. Vechnaya pamyat!"[2] he exclaimed. Then drained his glass in a gulp.

"Vechnaya pamyat!" everyone cheered in unison.

As the evening wore on, and the plates grew empty, the sun was beginning to disappear behind the surrounding hills. Yelizaveta enlisted the help of Savka and Tatyana and cleared the table.

"Everyone, go to the living room, and I'll bring tea," instructed Yelizaveta.

Victor got up from the table and stopped to take in another glance of the great view the window offered. With dusk approaching, the shadows grew long. For a moment, he enjoyed the sunset, and then he saw them. Though barely visible, and nearly five hundred meters

---

[2] Let him be remembered forever.

away, he could make out the shapes of six armed men hurdling the trench, coming from the enemy side of the trench line; from the Luhansk People's Republic (LPR). Whirling around to leave, Victor glanced at Vasyli and said in whisper that only the old man could make out, "We have unwelcomed guests."

Vasyli gave an encouraging nod, then joining the others in the living room. It had long been a tradition in the Koval family to retire to the living room and regale each other with music and a story over tea. The living room doubled as Anna's playroom. As the busy feet rustled from room to room, some of her toys got kicked around.

"My dolly!" cried Anna cried in desperation.

"I'll get it," said Pavel. Picking up her and the doll, he sat in his high-back chair. Then he looked down at her little fingers around her doll, and sighed.

"Play something for us," requested Yelizaveta.

"Yes, play us a melody," added Vasyli, "a Ukrainian one."

"Okay," said Tatyana. She walked to her room and returned with a music case. She set it on the dining room table and took out a shiny dark, maple-colored violin. Lifting the sixteen-ounce package of polished wood and strings, she notched it under her chin. Then, with a bit of stage fright, she drew the horsehair of the bow across the strings. Like a living organism, the violin's silvery voice swelled, conveying the room to a settled serenity. For the next two minutes, the beauty of Tatyana's music took everyone's mind off the war. Anna swayed along with the movement of the bow. Yelizaveta closed her eyes, enraptured with the delicate humming of the reverberating air. Suddenly, an incongruous eruption of gunfire echoed outside, and the violin's sweet voice instantly fell silent, displacing the mirth of the moment. The sound of gunfire slammed into Pavel's brain like an icepick.

Then, with a look of frustration stemming from hundreds of such interruptions, Tatyana dejectedly put her violin back in its case.

"I'm sorry, my dear," said Vasyli.

"It was so beautiful," added Pavel. "I adore Skoryk's Ukrainian Melody! Thank you."

"Well, I suppose it's my turn?" asked Vasyli, grabbing a chair from the dining room. He waited for everyone to get settled. Savka sat on the floor with her back to the couch. For her, listening to grandpa was her due diligence to the family patriarch. Pavel slouched in his high-back chair, which was his throne and sanctuary. He held his two-year-old granddaughter Anna in his lap. She had done well during the meal, but was now getting tired and fidgety. Yelizaveta sat on the couch, along with Tatyana, Anton, and Fyodor. Everyone sipped their black tea, a regional favorite after dinner.

"Where's Victor?" asked Pavel.

"I sent him on an errand," replied Vasyli.

"This late?"

Grandpa offered no response, pretending not to hear. This was one of his favorite ploys he used to his advantage. Approaching his eighties, Vasyli felt he was in the December of his life. His great concern was now for the future of his family, and his country. Though nearly an octogenarian, his undiminished strength often surprised others. Vasyli cleared his throat and sat down. "In light of all the weaponizing of history, allow an old man to regale you with a bit of our history. Mind you, it's history without a spin. After all, as it is said, 'He that controls history, controls the future.'"

"Ha-ha, I'm intrigued," said Anton, stretching out his legs in front of him.

"Let it be said, from the earliest days of our history," continued Vasyli, "we've fought for our survival and freedom. As a people, down through the ages, we've been called various names: Little Russians, Ruthenians, Rusniaks, Ukies, and the like. Despite being a people, some even dare to call us an 'artificial country.' Yet, as the annals of history bear witness, we have been a people nonetheless; the people of the wild fields. Now, as the ancient Chronicler states, in the tenth century there was once a greedy prince named Igor.[3] Rapacious for land, he led an expedition against the ancient city of Byzantium. The expedition ended in disaster when his ships were destroyed with Greek fire. Nonetheless, Igor managed to extend his authority over the Turkic Pecheneg people, as well as the East Slavic tribe of the Drevlians. As a tyrant, he was renowned for collecting tribute. And though successful with the Pechenegs, Igor's attempt to extort more than was customary

---

[3] The Primary Chronicle of Kyivan Rus was authored by Nestor, an early Christian monk. Igor the Old (875-945 AD).

provoked the Drevlians. Under the crushing weight of such tyranny, the Drevlians sought counsel against him. And do you know what counsel they received?"

Tatyana shook her head. "No, tell us."

"Mal, the prince of the Drevlians said, 'When a wolf enters the sheepfold, you have to kill the wolf, or he'll slaughter all the sheep – one at a time,'" explained Vasyli.

"Wait, I know this one," interjected Fyodor.

"Don't interrupt," said Anton.

"No. It's quite alright," replied Vasyli.

"Well, when the greedy Igor came to collect, the people killed him. He was pulled apart by trees, if memory serves. Then, his queen, Olga, avenged his death in a most savage manner; she had all the Drevlian leaders slaughtered. Then she burned their capital. Have I got it right?" asked Fyodor.

"That's correct," replied Vasyli. "You might say this ancient tale underscores the reason why they call the steppeland *The Wild Fields*."

"But grandpa, what's the moral of the story?" asked Tatyana.

"The point is: freedom, next to religion, has been the motive for good deeds, as well as every evil under the sun. In every age, freedom has been beset by such natural enemies as lust for conquest, the strong man's craving for power, and the poor man's craving for bread."

"I don't understand," said Tatyana. "What do you mean freedom is beset?"

Vasyli waved his clenched fist. "I mean, the purest form of tyranny maintains the appearance of freedom. Do you see? All tyranny is bad, but the worst variety of it works with the machinery of freedom."

"I didn't realize your father was such an idealist," said Anton, slapping Pavel's knee.

Pavel took in the scene, watching the others, mesmerized by his father's tale.

"I just like history. And for it to be meaningful, it has to be interpreted," said Vasyli.

"Consider, it was under the very auspices of 'freedom' that Moscow sent 'little green men' into the Crimea to 'protect' the citizens of the *Russkiy Mir*."[4]

"To the Kremlin, the Crimeans were merely Russians outside of Russia."

"This is a civil war, not a war against Russia," said Fyodor in a respectful tone.

Vasyli laughed. "Really? Where did you read that? Invading to protect Russians outside of Russia is a pretext for war used many times before. It was Stalin's *causi belli* for the invasion of Poland in 1939. Besides, the situation here in the Donbas is remarkably like Crimea. Under the same pretext to rescue Russians outside of Russia..."

"Euromaidan was a fascist junta; a coup d'état against Yanukovych," snapped Fyodor.

"My dear young friend, that is the Russian narrative," said Vasyli. "Do you know the Russian narrative? It goes

---

[4] Russian World.

something like this: Russia says, 'we began in Kyiv, then went to Moscow. Nonetheless, Kyiv is a Russian city.' This is an extremely successful narrative."

"Ha-ha!" laughed Anton.

"Don't you see? The Russian narrative is prostitution! Sheer prostitution! As contradictory as a Sadducee conjuring up a ghost," roared Vasyli.

"Maidan woke Ukraine up from its slumber. It made us conscious again of our identity," continued Vasyli. "But we know we can lose it again, just like we did under the hammer and sickle."

"But what can we really do about what's going on?" asked Anton, with a dismissive wave of his hand.

"We can take a stand and fight," replied Vasyli.

"On which side?" pressed Fyodor.

"That should be obvious," said Vasyli. "The separatists say, 'Give us power to free you from these 'oppressors,' and we'll give you everything they never could."

"We certainly heard that!" seconded Tatyana.

"But the price is your freedom. And when none of their promises materialize, what you don't get is your freedom back. And if you complain about it, these 'liberators' crack your skull, put you in prison, or kill you," said Vasyli.

Pavel had contented himself to remain a bystander up to this point, but the combination of his father's increasingly intensifying rant, the stifling July heat, and Anna's squirming made him edgy.

"This is a young man's game. We're too old and have too much to lose," said Pavel, somewhat dismissively.

Vasyli looked at his son, shaking his head in disbelief.

"Yes, we must be patient...," corroborated Anton.

"If we don't take a stand now," said Vasyli as he stood up, "there will be nothing left to fight for."

"What about the Army? Why not let them do the job?" snapped Pavel, letting Anna slide out of his lap.

"The Army has done nothing but sit on their butts for the past six years!" remonstrated Savka, as she picked up Anna, "But you can't win a war by sitting on your ass."

"Savka, language!" exclaimed Yelizaveta.

"It's time for Anna to go to bed," said Savka.

"Okay dear," said Pavel, getting one more hug and kiss from Anna as she squirmed. Everyone followed suit, saying goodnight to little Anna.

"Vasyli," said Anton, "I appreciate your zeal, I really do, but Pavel is right. It's not our fight. Besides, I can't afford to think this idealistically. I spend most of my time under the earth, barely making ends meet."

"Make no mistake; this is our fight," said Vasyli, "and this is our watch."

"My friends, last year, our Ukrainian forces brought us back into the fold, but wolves remain in our midst. They're working for 'Mother Russia.' Their goal is to see 'Novorossiya'[5] become a reality. But this will never materialize. Their blindness is astounding! If the people of the Donbas could only see it."

---

[5] New Russia.

"Will anything make you leave?" asked Fyodor.

"I have lived here all my life, and I will die here," said Vasyli, as he sat back down.

Vasyli sighed. "The separatists call us fascists. They say we are puppets of the West. They ignorantly refer to us all as Banderivtsy.[6] Yet it is they who are the puppets; heeding the tune of Putin," stated Vasyli.

"So, is that it?" blurted Anton. "Must we be either pro-Russian or pro-Ukrainian? Nothing in between?"

"If there's fighting to be done, it should be the Army," declared Pavel.

"That's just the sort of sentiment the separatists are counting on," retorted Vasyli.

"Pavel, where do you stand in all of this?" asked Fyodor.

The room grew silent, as everyone looked at him for a reply.

"I'm pro-myself," said Pavel, snarkily.

"Ha-ha," laughed Anton.

Vasyli smiled and shook his head.

"Pavel, do you like your Vyshyvanka shirt?[7] Oh course you do," said Vasyli. "Wearing one under the Soviets could send you to a work prison. My grandfather Petro, died in a work camp in 1955. What was his crime? When the people lived under the Nazis, his village asked him to be their work foreman. But when the Red Army rolled

---

[6] Followers of the right-wing ideology of Stepan Bandera, who conspired with the Nazis against the Red Army in WWII.
[7] A traditional Ukrainian shirt.

back through, he was arrested for 'conspiring' with the Third Reich."

"My friends," sighed Vasyli, "I've said a lot, but hear me, the only thing necessary for the triumph of evil, is for good men to do nothing."

Then, quoting the national anthem, Vasyli invoked the words, "Ukraine is not yet dead, nor its glory and freedom. Luck will still smile on us my friends. Our enemies will die, as the dew does in the sunshine, and we, too, we'll live happily in our land."

"We fought the Nazis. Before that, we played the hunger games of the Holodomor.[8] That's what the hammer and sickle stand for: death and starvation. We survived the hammer of Stalin and the anvil of Hitler. We'll survive Putin as well. Furthermore, as long as we survive, Ukraine lives on, as the poet has said, 'in each pulse-beat of her people's heart.'"

"Well, this is all too rich for my blood," said Anton, standing up to take his leave. "The Kharchenko brothers were this patriotic too, but look where they ended up. Ah that's right, we don't know."

"I love history," said Fyodor, joining him. "It's always refreshing to hear it, especially when it's told with such zeal," he added with a bow.

Anton and Fyodor thanked their hosts and bid all a goodnight. With their guests gone, the family was free to go about their nighttime rituals. Soon, Pavel and Yelizaveta were left in the living room alone.

---

[8] Russian for: death by hunger.

Now that he was alone with his wife, Pavel felt he could safely take off the proverbial mask he had worn for others.

"History is but the record of human crimes and misfortunes," said Pavel.

"Despite what my father says, I still want to leave."

"Really?"

"Terribly. I think if we're going to get out, now is the time... before it's too late," he said anxiously.

"To live with your sister in Odessa?"

"To start... we'd eventually get a place of our own."

"Start over you mean? We're too old to start over!"

"I know that doesn't sound very good. I just don't see a future for us here," he replied.

"Leaving is like rafting out to sea," she said, "besides, what about your father's butcher shop?"

"Look, there's a lot my father didn't say. To his litany, I could add feckless police, rogue militias, mafia, corrupt politicians, errant bullets, and a whole lot more in between!"

Pavel leaned in close to his wife's face. Her fish scale blue eyes functioned like mood rings. He could always tell her emotional disposition by them, which had become anxious and annoyed.

"Look, I'm no coward," he said.

"I know that!"

"My father thinks we have a future here, but we don't. The only future we have here is tyranny – and a bloodbath. We've got to get out before it's too late!"

"What about the girls?" she asked.

"They're here only because we are. They'll have a new life too... far away from here!" he said, trying to convince her.

"What has your father said about this?"

"He hasn't... I mean, I haven't told him yet. How can I tell him?"

"What if I don't want to go?" she said.

"Weren't you at the funeral? That boy in that casket could have easily been Tatyana, or Savka, or even Anna! Do you really want to see that?" he said.

She nodded her head in agreement, then rubbed her hands together.

"What would it be like to take a stroll together in a park without the fear of an errant bullet killing us?" pressed Pavel. "Or how about Anna's schooling? Do you really want her to go to school here? They have sandbags covering the windows!"

"Okay, okay," she said reluctantly. "Then.... let's go." Feeling a sense of elation, Pavel leaned over on the couch, hugging his wife. "Thanks be to God," he thought with a sigh. For a long moment, he held her, then leaned in for a kiss. "Thank you, my love. Thank you." Yelizaveta got up to go to bed. "Are you coming?"

"I just want to read a bit," he said, as he pulled his white and blue embroidered vyshyvanka shirt over his head, giving out a sigh of relief.

"Okay," she said.

Pavel picked up what was left of his now lukewarm tea, settled back in his chair, and took a sip. He picked up his Bible and sat it in his lap. Shuffling reverently through the pages, he came to the place, then began to read: "The race is not to the swift, nor the battle to the strong, nor bread to the wise, nor riches to men of understanding, nor favor to men of skill; but time and chance happen to them all."

"Time and chance," he thought, "we really have control over nothing? The more I want control," he mused, "the less it seems I have."

Pavel closed his Bible and prayed: "Lord.... I haven't prayed to You... in quite some time... words escape me. Please show me what to do."

He felt he should pray more, but not knowing what to say, he closed with the Lord's Prayer: "For Thine is the kingdom, and the power, and the glory, forever. Amen."

He sat in the living room for another thirty minutes or so. His thoughts of leaving were suddenly interrupted by the muffled sounds of an intense gun battle raging outside. It was close.

"We have to leave. Only then will I be free from the war."

Yet, in many ways, Pavel felt as though he never left the war. In fact, it seemed to follow him wherever he went. He sighed, thinking of his father's diatribe. He wanted to express his patriotism too, especially when his father evoked the words of the national anthem: "Ukraine is not yet dead, nor its glory and freedom." Thinking of these words caused him to brim over with pride, but then he felt ashamed. Why was he reluctant to show his pride? He had always believed himself to be

Ukrainian; albeit, he thought, "what good would it do for him to join the side of the slaughter?"

There was simply too much to risk. He thought of Anna, Yelizaveta, and his daughters. His mind wandered also to the funeral and the young man in the casket. This reminded him of his greatest fear, one he dared not speak of: to see one of his children in such a cold box of death. He thought of little Anna. He couldn't bear the thought of it. Feeling destressed, his thoughts returned once again to moving, and what that would be like.

As he contemplated this, he heard the faint sound of a lullaby coming through the half-opened door down the hall; it was Savka, singing little Anna to sleep.

"What a beautiful voice," he thought, "and what a shame we have to argue all the time."

Things had been tense in the house ever since Savka moved back in. As his oldest daughter, Savka was a twenty-five-year-old living at home with her daughter. She had strong views on nearly everything, which was fine in themselves, but her views contrasted with nearly everyone else in the house. Yet, there was nowhere else for her to go, and he didn't wish for her to.

Despite the trouble, he did his level best to hold the family together, loving all his girls equally. Walking down the hall, he caught a glimpse of several oil paintings hanging in his father's room: rudimentary landscapes of various pastoral scenes and a self-portrait in the style of Leonid Mezheritski. However, it was the scent of the linseed oil wafting from the palette that served to conjure within him a moment in his youth. He smiled, taking in the fragrant trace which transported him back to an earlier time of innocence. He then continued down the hall, arriving just as Savka was laying Anna in her crib.

"In time to steal a good night kiss?" he inquired.

"Just made it," whispered Savka.

Pavel took his granddaughter in his arms. He held her close, kissing her cheeks. She squirmed to move, avoiding his chin whiskers.

"I love you, Anna," he breathed.

Then, he asked himself, "Will Savka give me trouble in leaving? Would she go along? He couldn't bear the thought of not having Anna and Savka in his life. He wouldn't think about it. He would find a way to make it all work.

"Goodnight, Anna. Goodnight sweetheart," he said to Savka, hugging her.

Walking to his room, he thought, "There are two people in me: one ready to cut and run, and the other desiring to be the good man in the tale confronting evil. The question is: Who will win?"

3

A Secret Meeting

Things were getting quieter in the Donbas, albeit more violent. This paradox was the norm for living along the line of contact after sunset. Night was falling, and the last light of the setting sun outlined the face of a man in an office, sitting in a high-back leather chair. The seated man, who might have been anywhere between fifty-five and sixty, had a square-cut goatee, and salt and pepper hair. His steel-gray eyes glistened forth a radiance of both ferocity and pain. The man took out a cigar, bit the end, and spit a clump of tobacco on the floor. He struck a match, illuminating others like sentry dogs behind him.

The man took several puffs of his cigar. "Weren't the instructions clear enough?" asked the man asked with a feral grin.

"Set the mine on the path, the useful idiot will walk down it at the precise time, and the POM-Z will do the rest?"

"It failed to detonate," replied a young man, who'd been standing in front of the seated man for quite some time in an uncomfortable silence.

"It was supposed to look like mortar fire, and..."

"I didn't know what to do," interrupted the young man.

"The wonderful thing about the POM-Z antipersonnel mine," continued the man with the cigar, "is that it creates a crater similar in shape to the 82millimetermortar."

"It didn't detonate!" said the young man, shrugging his shoulders.

"So, you shot him in the head? It's supposed to look like the Army did it!" said the man, laughing boisterously. But then, just as abruptly as his laugh erupted, he became deadly serious.

"How would that look like mortar fire? I can have any dummy shoot another dummy."

"Mr. Baranov, I can fix this," remonstrated the young man, growing increasingly distressed.

"And how would you do that?"

"I...."

"You've done quite enough already. Now, I've got to fix your mess," replied Mr. Baranov.

"Who have you told about this?" asked another man in the room.

"No one."

"A girl? Family?" drilled another.

"Not a soul."

A long pause ensued.

"Go home," said Baranov. "I'll call on you again when I need you."

The young man breathed out a sigh of relief, bowed his head, and then closed the door behind him as he left.

"Follow him... and finish him," ordered Baranov.

"The next time you see him, it'll be in a casket," said another man as he left.

"Huh, that's one way to get people to go to church. Before we're through, they'll be many more funerals in Zolote," said Baranov.

The door opened and closed again. Then, rising from his chair, Baranov tugged on a lamp pull chain, illuminating those in the room.

"Gentlemen, please have a seat," he said as he took a pull on his cigar and smiled.

"As you can see, the business of war mandates that we dispense of problems as they arise."

Vadim Baranov was a covert ops old hand, with experiences ranging from the Soviet-Afghan War to the Second Chechen War. During the Soviet gamble in Afghanistan, he served in Russia's elite Alpha Group. While his exploits in Afghanistan were renowned, perhaps his greatest claim to fame occurred in Lebanon.

It was September 1985. Hezbollah had kidnapped four Russian diplomats in Beirut. A message from the terrorists warned that the four Soviet captives would be executed, one by one, unless Moscow pressured pro-Syrian militiamen to stop shelling positions held by Hezbollah in Lebanon's northern city of Tripoli.

Initially, Moscow attempted to open channels of communication in hope of negotiating the release of the hostages. However, after the militants executed one of the Russians, the Kremlin sent in Alpha Group. The Soviet operatives nabbed a dozen or so Shi'a militants to even things out; among one of whom was the relative of a Hezbollah leader. Vadim castrated the relative and shot him in the head, then stuffed his testicles in his mouth. He then shipped his body to Hezbollah with a letter promising a similar fate for the other eleven Shi'a captives, if the Soviet hostages were not released.

The show of force was vicious yet effective, and the message was received. In fact, it was so effective that, following Beirut for about twenty years, no Soviet or Russian officials were ever taken captive.

Besides past exploits such as these, Vadim was a social chameleon of the first order. Charm was his form of camouflage, which served to thinly veil a dispassionate ferocity underneath. Sitting down with five others, he took another pull from his cigar, set it on an ashtray, and rested his arms on the table.

"I've come to terms with the police chief. I've found him to be a... let's say, a reasonable man," said Vadim, as he picked up a box of cigars and held it out.

"I hope that didn't cost you too much," replied Dimitri, as he took one, trimmed the end, and lit it. The table erupted in laughter.

"These policemen are either drunk or corrupt," said Dimitri.

Dimitri Litvinov had also served somewhere in the Afghan War and was just as callous and brutal as Vadim. Moreover, like Vadim, he was a first-rate manipulator, seeing people for what he could get out of them. He was also a first-rate skirt chaser. Vadim had spotted his talents early on, and the two became partners in crime.

"Let's just say it's now open season on the Banderivtsy.[1] No more POM-Zs. From here on out, we're limited only by our imagination. Gorgan will tie up this loose end. He's done well to deplete the Banderivtsy population. Even now, without a Banderivtsy militia around, the problem is that things have become too neutral. In the Afghan War, our solution to settling the stalemate was to artillery strike the cities and towns into submission. This, of course, kept the mujahideen out of the urban areas, but then the people from the cities swelled their ranks."

Vadim took a pull from his cigar. Then, a short burst of muffled gunfire erupted somewhere down the street. "Every war begins like a vibrant young man, full of piss and vinegar; much like that halfwit. Yet, without a fair degree of acrimony, friction, and chaos, war wheezes and dies like a tired old pensioner. Starting a war is easy,

---

[1] Pro-Russian slang for Nationalists.

finishing one is often difficult, and this war has grown to be quite boring. Albeit, the trick is, as with any covert op, to keep things small and manageable."

"Now, gentlemen, before we discuss tonight's business, what news?"

"Well, I'll start," said Dimitri. "Today, I learned of a certain Banderivtsy radio broadcast. We believe it's originating out of Zolote. It's shaping up to be a lot like the one we uncovered in Popasna."

Glancing at his notepad, he read, "Tryzub 101.7 FM." "I listened to about ten minutes of it today. Typical nationalistic rhetoric. His basic message was 'Novorossiya' is the people's false savior. What I found particularly interesting was what he said about kopankas."[2]

"Let's see," said Dimitri, finding the place in his notes, "kopankas are a sidelined energy source. While they provide cheap sources of heat, they endanger the government's plan to consolidate the region's coal producing industry."

"Sounds to me like they don't appreciate you employing their citizens?" asked Dimitri.

"Then, oh let's see, oh yes, our mysterious radio broadcaster went on to say that the separatists are merely Putin's puppets... oh, and here's my favorite part... our mysterious radioman summarized everything by saying, 'if we don't take a stand now, there will be nothing left to fight for.'"

---

[2] Unregulated coal mines.

"Ignorance in action! Not very original," said Vadim.

Inspired by the movie Reservoir Dogs, Vadim gave each member of his clandestine team a color code, forming *The St. George Circle.*

Dimitri, Vadim's intelligence chief, was referred to as Mr. Blue. He owned a nightclub in the nearby town of Hirske. Among Dimitri's patrons were off-duty Ukrainian soldiers.

"We'll find this rogue radioman, and when we're through with him, he'll discover whether or not he can stand," said Dimitri, dragging his index finger across his neck.

"Oh, and regarding tonight, nine o'clock until five minutes after is the window," said Dimitri.

"How did you come by that information?" asked Symon Rudenko, a store manager in Zolote 4. Known as Mr. Yellow, Symon managed to wordsmith some rather crafty pamphlets that could be found plastered all over Hirske and Zolote. His 'journalism' was decidedly yellow.

"My friend, you simply paint a picture; one trick at a time," said Dimitri, with a wink.

"We don't need binoculars, you see? These stupid soldiers get a little tipsy, and then tell a skirt everything. In just five nights of work, my ladies acquired a pattern of life for nearly the entire sector's worth of trench line! Oh, and the beauty is, the schedule never changes," said Dimitri, with a grin.

"Then, there's the opportunity we have with the Romani settlement. The people want them gone," said Dimitri.

"And so do I," said Vadim, with callous brevity. Dimitri looked down into his glass of vodka. "Last Friday, the police responded to an attack on their camp. Six men dressed in black, hurled Molotovs that burned two shanties to the ground. When the police arrived, the Romani refused to file a complaint."

"How many of them are there?" asked Mr. Yellow.

"About forty-five. Fifteen are of fighting age."

"They're a tool ripe for the yielding," said Mr. Yellow.

"What do you propose?" asked Vadim.

"All we need to do is channelize their grievance. The Romani can't afford to leave, and the people want them gone. All we need to do is arrange a flashpoint. I'll come up with a plan," said Dimitri.

"What about the church? What does the church have to say?" questioned Vadim.

"Two-thirds of the Ukrainian church remains with the Moscow Patriarchate. As for us, we fight for the hearts and minds of the remainder," said Father Mitka Blok, a Russian Orthodox priest.

Referred to as Mr. White, Father Mitka's sacerdotal presence bolstered recruitment of the people's Druzhina.[3] Within the last six months alone, he had brought in over twenty new recruits.

---

[3] Pro-Russian militia.

Despite the benefits of his involvement in giving the clandestine network something of a church sanctioning, as the most conscientious of The Circle, Father Mitka was a rather strange fit. What particularly bothered him was Vadim's presupposition of 'the end justifies the means.' Additionally, the priest winced at the murder of The Circle's victims, preferring to think of them as killings. However, what irked him most was when Vadim would say, 'Let the Banderivtsy suffocate in their own excrement.'

Then, there were the other shadowy aspects of The Circle's machinations, such as its black-marketing: The war in the Donbas created a new market for extremist groups in Europe, Africa, and the Middle East. Tons of weapons of all calibers, explosives, along with rocket-propelled grenades (RPGs), and the like, were exported to other conflict zones, such as Syria and Libya. Not to mention the prostitution and kidnapping; all of which kept Father Mitka up at night. This, coupled with the frequency of the recent bloodletting of the young Taras, now taxed his already heavy-laden conscience. Nonetheless, the warning voice of his conscience went unheeded.

He felt as though he was Herod Antipas, and his conscience was John the Baptist. The warning voice of his conscience cried out, and yet he imprisoned it. The frightful baying of his conscience was not unlike a bloodhound pursuing the evil deed of indifference. The question was, would he eventually behead his conscience?

Upon infiltrating the Luhansk Oblast, and his initial forays into laying the foundation of The St. George Circle, throughout his myriad of meetings and conversations, Vadim learned of Father Mitka's pro-Russian sympathies.

What sparked his interest was the fact that the Russian Orthodox Church had severed ties with Constantinople over proposing the independence of the Ukrainian Church. As a first-rate manipulator, Vadim then lured the priest into his web under the auspices of reclaiming these wayward congregations. It was, for Vadim, a brilliant piece of manipulation.

"I suppose," added Father Mitka, "what the church has to say is: Time discovers truth. The churches that are not siding with us now, will do in time."

"What of Father Malashenko?" questioned Vadim.

"He is a special case. The people of Zolote respect him. He filled a vacuum after his predecessor left," said the priest, reluctantly.

"Where is he from?" asked Dimitri.

"Mariupol, I think. But he is not political."

"But is he reasonable?" asked Vadim.

"For his sake, I hope he is. Dozens of churches have been drawn back into the Russian fold. Yet, his congregation is a holdout," said the priest.

"Never underestimate the power of faith and firepower! With God's blessing," said Vadim, with a light thump of his hand on the table, "we shall do our duty in gathering the scattered sheep."

"Amen," said the priest, crossing himself.

"Well, I'm happy to report the acquisition of the Donvaska and Dobrobilska mines awaits only a funds transfer," said Ivan Stakhanov, who managed The Circle's finances. As the manager of the Hirske branch of Krupsbank, he had a natural cover. Moreover, he was appropriately referred to as Mr. Green.

"How did you convince them?" asked Vadim.

"Let's just say, they realized that when the time comes, they'll be well inside the new lines."

"Splendid," said Vadim with a smile, accentuating the savage scar on his right cheek.

Mr. Green had been instrumental in helping Vadim acquire his new position as director of the Kobalt Mine; a position Vadim attained a mere two days before. Vadim's predecessor, Oleh Petrokov, had opposed the takeover. Petrokov saw the light of day when a bomb went off in his apartment. The whole affair was then absorbed into the fog of war.

"As for the kopankas, now that we've had our tenth one become operational, we're employing two hundred fifty-three miners," continued Mr. Green.

"What's the accrued revenue?" asked Vadim.

"Five thousand USD last month," replied Mr. Green.

"But that's five thousand not going the National Coal!" exclaimed Vadim. "When winter comes around again, the people won't soon forget who kept them warm!"

"Precisely! And there's more," added Mr. Green.

"What's that?" asked Vadim.

"We may have a new opportunity. Agrigroup is in debt up to their eyeballs. As far as grain and feed go,

Agrigroup supplies nearly all the farms east of Kharkiv," added Mr. Green.

"To whom are they in debt?" queried Vadim.

"China... Exim Bank. If we could acquire thirty percent of Agrigroup, we'd control its interest," said Mr. Green.

"How much are we talking about here?" asked Vadim.

"Four million USD," answered Mr. Green, plugging away at a calculator. "That's roughly... one hundred million hryvnia."

"I'll discuss it with the department team," suggested Vadim.

"Okay, that brings us to local issues," said Mr. Green.

"As far as payroll, with the network now at just over two hundred persons, a journalist, an OSCE representative, and the mayor," he said, with a smile, "sector funding now exceeds just over fifty thousand USD... that's a million hryvnia a month. With two weeks to go before our next scheduled deposit, we're tapped out."

"Our journalist has done exceedingly well. Last week, he filed a complaint with the police regarding what he called SBU[4] fascist tactics, violations of freedom of press, and so on," said Dimitri.

"The question is," added Dimitri, "when are we going to get something out of this mayor?"

"I'd say, by his indifference, we have," replied Mr. Yellow.

"For five thousand USD a month?" remarked Dimitri.

---

[4] Security Service of Ukraine (SBU).

"What do you propose?" asked Vadim.

"I'm not sure. I'd just like to get our pound of flesh out of him."

"I'm sure we'll figure it out," said Vadim.

"As for getting paid," added Vadim, "everyone will just have to wait until after the dust settles. Fair enough?"

"Anything else? Okay, then let's go through it one more time," said Vadim before, placing a map of Zolote on the table and rolling it out. Pointing at the village of Partyzansky, Vadim ran his finger west four hundred meters to a position at about the midway point on the line of contact between the village and the Ukrainian Army strongpoint.

"After Mr. Pink has finished disposing of our young friend, he'll link up with our contacts tonight at nine o'clock here. They'll come through Pervomais'k. Alexei will have the package. Two others will haul the rockets. Veles will guide them through the minefield; they'll cross the trench line here, traverse these fields using the hedgerows as concealment, then cross over the rails here, and then, go a bit further up to this point on the road. The pick-up point is here."

"I'll have a passenger van standing by," confirmed Petro Shevchenko. Codename Mr. Brown, he managed a commercial moving company in Severodonetsk.

"Once we get an up, I'll drop them off at Site 2," added Mr. Brown.

"The church has furnished the site with food and water," said Father Mitka.

"I'll be on-call in case I'm needed," said Dr. Bohdan Melnyk. Codename Mr. Red, Melnyk was a doctor at the hospital in Hirske.

"Tomorrow morning at nine o'clock, I'll take them to the barn," said Mr. Brown.

"Then, we all meet back here Tuesday night," said Vadim.

"Everyone got it? Once I'm back from the sector command, we'll finalize things for the rest of the week," said Vadim while, taking another pull on his cigar.

"Tonight," continued Vadim, "we'll receive our guests, and by the end of the week, we'll take back this town! Any questions?... good."

"The longer we drag things along, the wider the gap with Kyiv grows! All we have to do is survive, and we win!" exclaimed Vadim, raising his glass. "To the gap with Kyiv!"

"To the gap!" replied the group.

With the meeting over, those in attendance paced their departure by several minutes apart. Soon, only Dimitri and Vadim were left.

"A year's worth of work is about to be rewarded. How do you feel?... You don't seem ecstatic," asserted Vadim.

"Are you sure Alexei is bringing the funds?" asked Dimitri.

"Yes."

"I can't help but be concerned."

"About what?"

"Do the others suspect?" asked Dimitri, knitting his brow.

"You worry too much, my friend. Leave it to me. Alexei will be carrying the funds. The others have the rockets. With the funds, we'll acquire these other mines, and anything else that will prove lucrative, and when the dust settles, we'll come out on top," said Vadim as he looked at his friend. He didn't seem assuaged.

"We haven't done anything this big before," said Dimitri.

"Leave it to me," encouraged Vadim.

For the moment, this seemed to satisfy Dimitri's angst. The two men got up to leave. As Vadim tugged downward on the lamp pull chain, the report of a single bullet piercing the night air could be heard.

As the two left the office, Vadim closed the door and said, "You never know where the angel of death may strike."

4

Where the Militias Roam

Necessary for the stability and survival of any nation is its sovereignty and borders. Lying at the crossroads of Europe, Ukraine has long struggled to forge an independent path between the West and Russia. So great has been this conflict that a prominent theme in Ukraine's history is its struggle for freedom from foreign rule. Though often challenged, the modern Ukrainian state traces its roots to the Cossack Hetmanate. Also known as the Zaporizhian Host, the Cossack Hetmanate existed for over a hundred years, from 1648 to 1764.

That the Cossack Hetmanate is the origin of the modern Ukrainian nation may be argued etymologically and spiritually. In the first sense, Ukraine was the name the Ottomans used to describe the Cossack Hetmanate. Likewise, the Poles referred to Ukraine as the Land of the Cossacks. Moreover, in the spiritual sense, Cossack hetmans allied themselves with both the West and East in the struggle for freedom. In 1654, Hetman Bohdan Khmelnytsky signed a treaty allying the Cossack people with Russia against Poland. Demonstrating the East-West struggle, another Cossack hetman, Ivan Mazepa, sided with Sweden against Peter the Great of Russia.

Under the hammer and sickle, Ukraine's identity faded into the backdrop of communism. The evil nature of communism was that it masked everyone it infected with it. Despite the strangulating hold of Marxist-Leninist ideals, the genocidal tactic of Holodomor,[1] and the scourges of two World Wars, Ukraine lived on in the lifeblood of its people.

Following the collapse of the Soviet Union in 1991, the nation was faced yet again with the ancient question posed by its geopolitical positioning of whether to side with the East or the West. The question came to a flashpoint in February 2014, after the then-President Yanukovych, under pressure from Moscow, in a last-minute decision, scrapped plans to formalize a closer economic relationship with the European Union. Protests immediately erupted in Kyiv's Maidan square.

---

[1] Russian for: death by starvation. This was the name given for the man-made famine of Stalin's ruthless regime in 1932-1933, which killed some ten million Ukrainians.

Tensions rose as numbers in the Maidan increased. The powder keg ignited when Yanukovych sought to crush the protests, allegedly giving the order to fire on protesters. However, this drew an even greater number of protesters, prompting Yanukovych to flee the country. Then, in March 2014, Putin exploited the political vacuum by sending his secret army into the Crimea. Referred to as little green men for their lack of insignias of any type, Putin's private army seized government and police buildings, while Moscow denied their existence. The effectiveness of this hybrid form of warfare was underscored by the speed of events it engendered. In under two weeks, Putin organized a referendum at gunpoint, then annexed the Crimea under the pretense of protecting Russian citizens.

In the fallout, the Euromaidan protests and Crimea crisis exacerbated the ethnic tensions in the Donbas. Within two months of Russia annexing the Crimea, pro-Russian separatists in the Donetsk and Luhansk regions followed suit. Following Putin's playbook, beginning April 12, 2014, in Donetsk City, pro-Russian militants seized government buildings, barricaded themselves inside, and then demanded independence.

Similarly, separatists in Mariupol, Sloviansk, Luhansk, along with other major cities, likewise did the same. Organized by Russian GRU agents, such as Igor Girkin and Igor Bezler, separatists followed similar tactics all over the Donbas, destabilizing city centers. Making matters worse for the government, officials in many cities and towns, including Ukraine's Berkut riot police, sided with separatists.

The militant's playbook went as follows: First, they seized control of city and government administrative buildings. Then, they would demand autonomy and amnesty for all protesters. After which, they would gather a 'people's assembly' to vote for a referendum of independence from Ukraine. Moreover, to bolster their fighting strength, militants moved to seize army and police weapon caches. Finally, to solidify their holdings, on April 27, 2014, the people of the Donetsk and Luhansk Oblasts declared the self-styled Luhansk and Donetsk People's Republics (LPR and DPR).

In response, acting Ukrainian President Oleksandr Turchynov vowed to reclaim the Oblasts in what he referred to as an "Anti-Terrorist Operation" against the insurgents. Initially having been caught off-guard, Ukrainian troops swiftly moved to repatriate several cities and towns of the Donbas, making headlines in the recapture of Sloviansk. With this new zeal, Ukrainian forces seemed unstoppable, at least until the Russian media whipped the Russian-speaking peoples of the Donetsk and Luhansk Oblasts into a frenzy.

In dire straits, Igor Girkin also petitioned Putin for military support to protect the fledgling pro-Russian republics against what Girkin referred to as "the threat of NATO intervention." Having gained a new influx of Russian men and materiel, insurgent forces flexed forward, culminating in May and June of 2014, when fighting between government and separatist forces escalated. In the frontline tug-of-war, hostilities centered on the Sergei Prokofiev Airport in Donetsk, which was left annihilated.

Then, the conflict became an international flashpoint when the passenger jet, Malaysia Airlines Flight 17, was shot down on July 17, 2014, killing all two hundred ninety-eight people on board. While separatists blamed the Ukrainian Army for the disaster, the governments of the Netherlands and Australia blamed Russia and her proxies. Following the downing of the Malaysian jet, Ukrainian forces retook Severodonetsk and Popasna. On this momentum, government forces broke through the insurgent blockade near Donetsk airport before advancing, then advanced into Donetsk city.

As the fighting intensified, the battle for Donetsk City began to resemble the great urban battles of WWII. Massive artillery barrages were followed by savage close-quarters combat for the control of each street. Following a series of insurgent defeats, Igor Girkin urged more Russian military intervention, and addressed Russian president Vladimir Putin, saying, "Losing this war on the territory that President Putin personally named New Russia would threaten the Kremlin's power and, personally, the power of the president."

Fighting along the frontline continued until everything ended with an entrenched standoff. Then, a ceasefire was called on September 5, 2014. In a show of clemency, President Petro Poroshenko then offered the breakaway republics a special status in which the Russian language would be protected by law.

Notwithstanding these and other concessions, DPR and LPR leaders avowed their desire for full independence from Ukraine. For them, there would be no way back into the fold.

Further entrenching both sides, the February 2015 Minsk agreement called for Ukrainian and separatist forces to withdraw from the ceasefire line. While aspects of the ceasefire, such as a prohibited use of artillery, as well as drones, would prove beneficial to the suffering civilians on both sides, these measures have yet to prove effective in ending the conflict. Over time, drones would evolve into a cost-effective means to fight war on the cheap.

This was underscored in living color in the summer of 2017, when a Russian drone caused huge collateral damage to a Ukrainian Army depot in Balakliya. Dropping a thermite grenade, the Russian drone caused some 20,000 people to be evacuated as dozens of blasts and secondary explosions rocked the city, leading to billions worth of losses. Following the ceasefire, the no - man's land between the long line of trenches became known as the 'gray zone.'

Split in two by this buffer, Zolote had been controlled by separatist forces since the summer of 2014. Following the wave of political sentiment that was enveloping the Donbas, Zolote mayor, Volodymyr Krotova, organized a referendum in support of the LPR, bringing Zolote into the *Russkiy Mir*. As the destructive force of the war raged around the town, many left while those too old to leave stayed. By the time the town was wrestled back by the Ukrainian army in 2018, trenches on both sides were hastily dug, splitting the town in two. At some points, trenches came as close as 100 meters apart. From above, commencing at the Sea of Azov, the trench line could be seen as a deep scar gouged into the soul of Eastern Ukraine. Dug about six feet into the black earth, and terminating near the Russian border, the trench line spanned some five hundred kilometers, dividing the self-styled Luhansk and Donetsk People's Republics (LPR and DPR) from the rest of Ukraine.

Since the beginning of the war, many units operating along the line of contact resembled the bands of marauding Cossacks that had made the wild fields infamous. Such were the Wolves' Hundred, a Russian paramilitary group. Thrusting west as far as Sloviansk, it was believed this group formed the original core of the separatist fighters who took over several towns in April 2014.

On the pro-Ukrainian side, such elements as the Azov Battalion, a Ukrainian National Guard unit that once helped to recapture Mariupol, served as a type of police unit on the far eastern edge of the line of contact. Adding to the milieu, men came from all over the world to fight on both sides. For instance, as in Mariupol, the war had drawn volunteer Muslim fighters from Chechnya. With no love loss for the Russians, these mujahideen threw in their lot in defense of Ukrainian soil. All along the line, contending for every square meter of turf, these fighting elements demonstrated the living breathing aspect of the line of contact, once again making the wild fields a truly dangerous place to live.

Following the ceasefire and Minsk agreements, life on the line of contact became reminiscent of the stalemate trench warfare of the First World War. However normalized the conflict had become, around Zolote, intermittent attacks became a daily occurrence, producing an average of two Army casualties every day. At times, tensions built up to a level that led to periods of intense fighting. Such clashes erupted along the line as various army and militia formations exchanged fire.

For example, early in 2019, separatists attacked Ukrainian forces at Zolote with heavy artillery, causing extensive damage. Then, in May, the Ukrainian 46th Assault Battalion advanced east of Popasna. The line of contact had encroached on the town. To add some breathing space, the unit pushed the gray zone a full kilometer deeper into the LPR.

Like other frontline towns, some residential buildings in Zolote became military positions. From this base of operation, local militia and National Guard elements could be rotated into the trench line, then returned to refit. Adding to the government's hardships on the frontline, in the earlier part of 2019, in order to fulfill part of its obligations under the Minsk agreement, Kyiv agreed to disband Ukrainian militias. This was a black day for these volunteers, as they had augmented the unprepared Ukrainian Army and no doubt stemmed the tide of the pro-Russian juggernaut. In the hay day of the volunteer battalions, there were some 15,000 citizens and foreigners in their ranks. One by one, the pro-Ukrainian militias were reluctantly disbanding. It was the last days of the volunteer battalions. These were days of high adventure.

два

It was Monday morning. As could be pieced together from various stories, the previous night a group of separatists attempted to cross the line of contact unnoticed. However, they were intercepted on a path that ran along a field just west of Partyzansky. Somehow, they were able to traverse the minefields unscathed. Running north in a file and silhouetted against a dark crimson sky, voices yelled at them, calling for them to halt. They froze. Eight men could be made out, as the sun silhouetted them on the horizon. Dressed in paramilitary attire of assorted type, they each carried a Kalashnikov and military-style packs. But as to their loyalties, it could only be assumed they were pro-Russian.

Those yelling for the group to stop were lying in the prone at a near right angle, some seventy-five feet away in a commanding position of higher ground that rose about ten feet above the path. They had hastily dropped into the prone with their guns out and at the ready. All were armed with AK-47s, except for one with a PKM, a Soviet light machine gun that fires 7.62 millimeter. Forming a line with about five feet separation, the six men poised themselves to attack. One man in the prone yelled out, "Drop your weapons! Hands up!"

"Drop your weapons!" said another man echoing. A long silent moment lapsed as the two groups faced each other. The tension could be felt. Then one man on the path turned, dropped to a knee, and opened fire. Letting out a quick burst, his AK-47 broke the silence – BRRAAAAAAW! His third and fourth rounds struck a man lying in the prone, hitting him in the groin and abdomen, causing him to breathe out a deep pain-filled groan.

This salvo was instantly answered by an eruption of fire from those uphill. Then for some thirty seconds, the area around the two groups of fighters, consisting of a hundred square meter field, was transformed into a virtual cauldron of flying lead. Those in nearby homes watched the numerous muzzle flashes and heard the distinctive report of the Kalashnikov. The PKM rattled away – DUH, DUH, DUH, DUH, DUH, DUH, DUH, DUH... The air above the field cracked, hissed, and banged forth a reverberating cacophony, as men yelled and cursed.

Of those on the path, three escaped the menacing fire, stumbling into a nearby creek, while the remaining five managed to return fire briefly before being cut down by the PKM that mercilessly clanked away. A cloud of gun smoke hovered just above those in the field as the PKM continued to hammer away – DUH, DUH, DUH, DUH, DUH, DUH...

Then a voice coming from among those along the high ground cried "Cease-fire!" The firing stopped like popcorn as the command was echoed. There was a long pause, then a voice on the high ground raised a shout, "Slava Ukraini!" At which everyone said, "Slava Ukraini! Heroiam slava!"[2]

In a clump of trees, some two hundred meters away, lay Gorgan. He had managed to avoid getting himself cut down in the ambush. Using the base of a tree as cover, he lay on his back, trying to catch his breath. Feeling a sharp pain, he felt a warm flow of blood as it pooled on his side. It was a graze. He breathed out a sigh of relief as he took stock of the situation. He found that he only had two others with him. Alexei was captured. Ukraine's militia had gotten the drop on Russia's ghost army.

Три

It was early Monday morning. Pavel and Vasyli arrived to ready the butcher shop for the business day. Soon afterward, Victor arrived and began helping Pavel chop various meats, getting them ready for the display. Noting some empty shelves, Vasyli set himself to the task of restocking. Pavel was happy to stay busy. His goal was to avoid his father, specifically any his father's diatribes involving the family business. He just wanted to get out altogether, but he just didn't know how to go about saying it. He entertained the idea of suggesting that

---

[2] "Glory to Ukraine. Glory to heroes."

perhaps Victor take over his position as co-proprietor; at least then he would feel better when he left.

"Did you hear what happened last night?" asked Victor, as he walked into the back of the butcher shop. He dropped a bag, washed his hands, and put on his apron for work.

"I heard a firefight. Who could miss it?" asked Pavel. Then, he thought, "If I can just keep busy, then no one will pester me."

"A group of traitors were slaughtered," Victor let out with a grin.

Pavel kept to his work, trying to avoid Victor, who was insistent on telling him the full story. As he thought through the news, Symon Rudenko entered the store.

"Hello, Symon. How are things with your mother?" asked Vasyli.

"She's doing well."

"Yes, she certainly is. With her diabetes flare-up, she looked to be at death's door. Thank God is with us!"

"Yes. Thank God."

"The usual? Let's see, thirty pounds of ground beef, five chickens, and four racks of lamb?"

"That's it."

"I have it all boxed. I was just waiting for you to arrive. Victor, take it out to his truck, would you?"

"Certainly."

"My friend, you must have gone through quite a lot of Hryvnia on that medicine. How are things?" asked Vasyli.

"Things were tight but now they're okay, my friend."

"And how about you my friend.... How are you making out?" asked Symon.

"Things are always good," said Vasyli, looking at Pavel, "when you've got family."

"Okay, friend," said Vasyli, as Victor came back in, "I'll send you the invoice."

"Good day to you all," said Symon.

Vasyli walked over to the front door, watching Symon get in his truck and drive off.

"Insulin is not easily obtained; not around here, anyway," said Pavel.

"I know. It must've cost him... and is costing him a small fortune," replied Vasyli.

Pavel and Victor went back to carving up a hog, while Vasyli stocked some shelves with canned goods.

"Four were found dead, and one is in the hospital, shot up pretty bad," said Victor.

"You don't say?" replied Pavel.

"Yeah, in fact, I bet he looks like that pork loin you're cutting up."

"Who were they?" asked Pavel, thinking "and where were you when all this happened?"

"Glad to hear someone is doing something about these separatists," said Vasyli, as he walked in the back.

"Who?" asked Pavel.

"Concerned citizens. It great to hear the people are taking a stand," replied Vasyli contently.

He stepped toward Pavel and put his hand on his shoulder as if to say, 'what do you expect?'

"But how do we know they were separatists?" asked Pavel.

"Well," said Victor, "there's one that's shot up and in the hospital. He was found with a satchel full of explosives and is Russian."

"What do you make of that, Pavel?" asked Vasyli.

Pavel continued to work quietly. "Not sure."

"This is more than the usual exchange of gunfire over the fields. I believe it means an enemy operation is imminent," said Vasyli.

Pavel filled two baskets full of packaged meats before washing, then washed his hands. He wouldn't let himself get caught up in this. Besides, he had already decided to leave town – and the Donbas to its fate.

"Where are you going?" asked Vasyli.

"To the church. I've got to deliver these meats to Father Malashenko. It's our offering," replied Pavel curtly.

"Oh, yes. Splendid," said Vasyli.

"While you're there, say a prayer for our dearly departed friend."

"I will, father. I'll be back in a half-hour."

Vasyli watched Pavel get into his truck.

"You were there?" asked Vasyli, stocking a shelf with cans of soup.

"Yes," said Victor.

"Well, what happened?"

"They crossed the trench line just west of your house."

"Really? They jumped the trench. That's new."

"How they got through the minefield is beyond me!" said Victor.

"When everyone went into the living room, I took another glance out of the window when I saw them. Then, I ran as fast as I could to Lev's garage. Most of the militia were still there having some beers. I told Lev where I saw them jump the trench. Then, we grabbed our guns and got into a position, hoping to intercept them."

"Did anyone see you?"

"No. I don't think," said Victor pensively.

"Then what?" asked Vasyli.

"We arrived just as they were walking through the field in between the tracks and the trench. We could make out eight of them... I think. My heart nearly burst out of my chest. Then, Lev gave the order to fire, and we cut them down! I must've got two with the PKM. I nearly went through two drums! After the smoke settled, we counted four bodies, and captured one. But I think a few got away."

"Who else knows?"

"Just our squad; and now you."

"Ok. Let's keep it that way. Be careful who you tell about this. The walls have ears."

"Artem got shot too. He's at the farmhouse," said Victor.

"Who's tending to him?"

"A doctor. His name is Melnyk, I think. He works at the hospital in Hirske. He made a house call."

"Do we know if we can trust him?"

"I don't know. But you should've seen him. Artem would have most certainly have died."

"What about the Russian?"

"He's in the hospital under police guard."

"What else did you find?"

"The smoke had not so much as settled over the field when we saw the police arriving. We left before they got there. None of us had enough time to search the bodies, but we did manage to grab their guns; four AKs.

"Okay, but we have to be extremely careful. The walls have ears – and eyes. As they say, 'it only takes a single leak to sink a whole ship.'"

5

Afgantsy[1]

For many veterans, it's a story of war finding them, yet never leaving them the same. War leaves an indelible mark on the soul. Pavel was one such veteran. He had walked out to his truck, intent on driving to the church, but ended up sitting quietly for several minutes. He got there in a hurry but then became lost again in his thoughts.

"Imminent enemy operation? Huh, then I'll have to leave sooner," he thought. He looked down at his hands

---

[1] Afgantsy is the Russian term for the Soviet soldiers who fought the Soviet-Afghan War. Afganets is singular.

and smelled them. A faint trace of blood lingered despite his many hand washings. He considered how much he loathed the town, the conflict in which it was now hopelessly enmeshed, the fragility of life, and contemplated how much better everything would be if he could only live someplace else. "Anywhere but here," he thought. He spent the better part of another ten minutes navel-gazing.

Out of nowhere, Stepan appeared, tapping lightly on the driver-side window. Pavel rolled it down and smiled at his old friend. Fresh from his work in the mines and soaked in sweat, Stepan was characteristically covered with coal dust from head to toe. His miner's helmet was tucked under his arm. The sweat of his face melted away most of the coal dust, leaving behind a residual line of miner's mascara.

"Afganets," said Stepan. "What are you doing?"

"Just delivering some things to the church."

"Looks like you're in deep thought to me. Your truck is still parked. What's on your mind?"

A long pause ensued.

"A wise man once said, 'we suffer more in imagination than we do in reality.' Do you believe that's true?" asked Stepan.

"I certainly do. I only wish I could apply the wise man's counsel to myself."

"Want a ride home?" offered Pavel.

"Sure."

"When are you going to get a car?"

"I suppose when you stop giving me rides."

Stepan's presence cheered Pavel up a bit. Pavel cleared the passenger seat of debris then leaned over to unlock the door. Stepan lived in a neighboring town only a few miles down the road, and so it was on the way to the church.

Stepan opened the door and climbed in the pickup truck; a two-door 1989 Mitsubishi. Letting the bag on his shoulder fall free onto the truck's floorboard, Stepan put his miner's helmet on his lap, and breathed out a sigh of relief. It appeared as though Pavel would start the truck, but after he put the key in the ignition, he paused.

"Do you ever dream about that day in Laghman?"

"Sometimes, I suppose."

"I go there every night in my dreams," said Pavel.

"The lush greenery of the terraced fields, standing starkly against the surrounding desert, beneath the towering mountains of the Hindu Kush. The sunbaked mud houses they've made there the same way for centuries, and the village that time seemed to forget... at least until the day we arrived."

A wave of fear rolled over Pavel as he went there in his mind. He closed his eyes and grit his teeth as his face winced with unseen pain.

It was two days after Christmas in 1979. Under the auspices of freedom, Moscow invaded Afghanistan using the same tried and true techniques they employed in the invasion of Czechoslovakia: a rapid seizure of major cities, police stations, and city councils, followed by airstrips and existing bases, until they had a controlling grip on the governmental administration centers. In this instance, the Russian invasion was prompted by the Kremlin's desire to protect its Soviet neighbor.

Afghanistan's previous government had been overthrown by those of the Marxist-Leninist People's Democratic Party of Afghanistan. The new government forged close ties with the Kremlin and launched extensive land and social reforms, provoking those strictly following sharia law. The government in turn set out to ruthlessly purge Afghanistan of all opposition.

Backfiring on the fledging Soviet government of Afghanistan, droves of fighting-aged male Afghans swelled the ranks of several insurgencies sworn to engage in jihad against the communist government and purge the infidels from the land. These holy warriors were collectively referred to as the Mujahideen.

In response, the goal of the Soviet invasion was to prop up their new puppet state. In the lightning coup, they executed Afghan President Amin in his Kabul palace, then foisted Babrak Karmal in his place. Fanning out to encompass every urban center, in motorized columns, the Soviets garrisoned the Afghan landscape.

Notwithstanding the Russian zeal, the mountainous terrain and the enemy were entirely different from what the Red Army had prepared for. Moreover, the structure of the Soviet forces, as well as the tactics they employed, were clearly ineffective. In a matter of months, the Red Army loathed the counter-guerrilla warfare that their 'glorious invasion' had devolved into.

Pavel was only eighteen years old when he was conscripted into the Soviet Army in 1983. He was one of half a million Soviet soldiers who would rotate through the landlocked nation on the roof of Asia. After his basic training, he was assigned to a motorized rifle company in Kabul. When he arrived, he felt like he had been sent to another planet. Built in the 1950s, the Soviet airbase in Kabul was situated at nearly six thousand feet above sea level. For the next ten years, the Soviet airbase served as the main hub in the struggle to subdue the Islamist insurgents.

Comprising of a single asphalt landing surface in what looked like a bowl surrounded by mountains, the Kabul airbase was its own little city, furnished with various gravel pathways that radiated out to tent cities. Along the perimeter of the airbase were numerous machine-gun nests and barbed wire fence defenses. Rising above the base, and on three sides, stood the majestic, treeless ridges. Then, farther to the east, high above the valley that ran eastward, were the snow-capped peaks of the Hindu Kush.

Like most conscripts, being from Ukraine, Georgia, or the so-called 'lesser republics,' Pavel performed any myriad of menial tasks. His company spent the better part of a year assigned to perimeter defense. This meant that, for most of his first six months, he dug fighting positions, filled sandbags, and spent countless hours staring at the mountains that ringed the airbase.

The monotony of security duty gave the soldiers of his company too much time on their hands. To fight the enemy of boredom, many Soviet troops resorted to drugs, which were in ample supply. Opium, heroin, and hashish could easily be obtained. Adding to the malignancy of such troops, their habit could be bankrolled through the selling of ammunition, equipment, and weapons. Demonstrating the debilitating effects of this malignancy, one company on the base had an incident in which one of its sergeants was fragged in his sleep. In a tuff over the affections of a female nurse, one soldier threw a grenade into the other sergeant's tent. Incidents like these were all too stereotypical.

As the spring of 1985 arrived, the war began its sixth year. Meeting Mujahideen ambushes with harsh reprisals, under Gorbachev, the Soviet 40th Army intensified its attacks on Afghan civilians. Soviet artillery barrages to clear villages of mujahideen were not uncommon. Then, in an attempt to clear the Kabul-Jalalabad Road, the Soviet command planned a series of sweeps. The action centered on Laghman Province, which lay east of Kabul. It was a region notorious for harboring insurgents.

When Pavel heard that his company had been selected to go on the operation, he was ecstatic; he would finally get off the base. This way, he thought, he could avoid typhoid, dysentery, or being fragged in his tent as he slept. His unit was to be a part of a combined force. Several motorized rifle companies in support of an airmobile commando strike force were given the task of raiding the village of Charbagh, which was believed to be crawling with mujahideen and enemy weapon caches.

Before sunrise, in the frosty morning early hours of April 8, 1985, a column of troops moved east toward Jalalabad, then turned north off the main artery. As they did, a snow-laden sky blew a strong wind into their faces. With menacing strides, the vengeful Soviet troops closed on the Pashtun village of Charbagh, which was ironically named for the garden paradise in the Quran. Built along the side of a hill, the ancient village straddled a wide, flattened spur offering a majestic commanding view of the Kabul River Valley. Towering above the village on three sides stood the lower reaches of the Hindu Kush.

The roar of the column could be heard for miles as the drum of the engines rebounded against the snow-capped, ringed hills. The BTR-70s belched their black diesel clouds as the ZIL-131 cargo trucks bore the troops in train. As the Soviet column strained uphill, coming into view, some Afghans fled their homes while most locked themselves inside.

Passing a downed and scavenged Soviet helicopter, the column came to an abrupt halt about two hundred meters from the first house. The troops then dismounted and fanned out in a half-moon around the southern end of the village. As they did, two Mi-8 Hips flew overhead. Clearing the ridge, the helicopters plunged into a steep descent, accentuating the changing pitch of the droning turbines and the whipping of the rotors. The distinctive clattering of their blades increased as they flared and landed, disgorging some twenty commandos. The distinct camo pattern of the commandos distinguished them from their 40th Army counterparts, who wore

Afghanka khakis. Pavel could even make out the blue and white striped telnyaska shirts they wore underneath their jackets.

The commandos wasted no time, breaking into homes by throwing grenades at the doors. From his position, Pavel could hear high-pitched screams, explosions, and gunfire. He glanced over to see a house on fire. Smoke billowed out of every orifice. A young child, no more than four, walked aimlessly out in front; her clothes stained with blood. Entering the homes systematically, the commandos looted and murdered their way from one side of the village to the other.

At blocking positions, the troops were instructed to shoot anyone running out of the village. Dozens of men and women were gunned down as they tried to escape the slaughter. With the massacre now in full swing, two Mi-24 Hind helicopters made gun runs. It was these storied gunships that came to embody the Soviet struggle in Afghanistan. Bursting over the ridge, they descended rapidly into the valley. Streaking low across the sky, the menacing craft raked fire on anything that moved. This was the year before the introduction of the Stinger missile, and Soviet pilots flew with impunity. Before long, the carcasses of cows, sheep, men, and goats littered the nearby rock-strewn fields.

By 7:30 am, the village was nearly engulfed in flames. Long, black flumes of smoke streamed hundreds of feet into the clear morning sky. Pavel and a few other troopers were then signaled to mount the bulldozers and backhoes their unit had brought along. They made short work of digging a jagged ditch, about four feet deep and a hundred feet long.

Other conscripts carried the bodies of Charbagh's dead villagers out of the houses and piled them up. Pavel now had a front-row seat for the grizzly business. Men, women, and children, young and old, lay in heaps. Some had been bayoneted; most had been shot.

Those shot bore the blackened signature of the close-range execution-style nature of their death – a single bullet to the forehead. Pavel saw three pregnant women. They had been bayoneted to death, they and their unborn. This, together with the nauseating stench of the burning bodies in the nearby houses, made Pavel's next task a grave one.

To his horror, he was directed to push the heaps of bodies into the long hole they had dug. Then, he saw him: an Afghan boy, no more than seventeen. His green kameez was stained with the blood flowing from his head wound. It was a graze. His red-orange hair seemed to be on fire in the morning sun, and his cerulean-green eyes glared in questioned astonishment. Pavel's eyes caught his just as a load of bodies rolled and tumbled into the ditch.

The boy wasn't dead, but he was spitting blood. He cried out something in Pashtun that Pavel didn't understand. Although he couldn't understand the words, Pavel felt as though something the boy said had power over him. It was as if the boy had invoked some sort of curse on him. Seeking some modicum of mercy, the boy held his guts with one hand while weakly flailing the other. From what Pavel could discern, his dozer blade had torn the boy open.

Seeing the boy's entrails spill out, and hearing his cries, had caused Pavel to bring his dozer to a screeching halt. He sat there like a stone, staring at the morose sight. As he did, one of the commando officers bellowed, "Hey, keep that machine moving!"

Pavel turned to see a commando captain resting a submachinegun on his shoulder.

"But Captain," said Pavel, "this one's alive."

"Really?"

The captain's piercing gaze caught Pavel's eye. Without hesitation, he leveled his RAK submachine gun, and, in an instant, shot the boy in the head. Pavel's guts heaved in horror. Then, the captain said callously, "You never know where the angel of death may strike. We all enjoy the sausage, but not everyone enjoys how it's made."

"Now, keep that machine moving," he bellowed, as he turned to leave.

Nodding reluctantly, and with a sickened feeling that soured in his guts, Pavel continued pushing the bodies into the ditch. By about eight o'clock, the grave work was done. The bodies of the slain lay under several feet of dirt, making the village something of a collective grave. Not long after, the commandos boarded up on their helicopters and flew off. No sooner had they left did the mujahideen arrived in the hills to the north of the village. They kept their distance but poured on a sustained rate of AK and RPG fire on the Soviet troopers in the village below. While their attack was not all that effective, their presence caused the Soviet column to withdraw in haste. As it did, Pavel glanced back at the long, shallow grave that he had made. The village was now completely engulfed in flames. It was later reported to have burned for four days straight.

Though Pavel never physically returned, every night, he revisited the village to see the horror, along with the questioning face of the murdered young man. Pavel now lived among others, and yet he was as distant and unfamiliar as the faraway away battlefields that haunted him.

"My friend. Brother," said Stepan, putting his hand on Pavel's shoulder. Pavel startled and shook, becoming aware again of where he was. He sat motionless for a long moment with his face fixed in a scowl.

"No matter what I do, I can't get that boy's face out of my head," said Pavel, breaking the silence.

"It's like every evil that has befallen me since, I can only think, is merely a repayment for my sins!" he continued, shaking his head in angst.

"It is said that, if you don't stand up against something you don't agree with, then you're complicit in permitting it to happen. Isn't that right?"

"You did your job, my friend," said Stepan, raising his palms and waving them skyward.

"I took part in a great murder – the murder of a whole village."

"War is hell, and the sure sign of our fallen nature. But war is also the best school of life. It brings out the best or worst in everyone. For us, that war was a defense of the Motherland. For Afghans, it was a defense of their religion."

"Was that war really worth the sacrifice?"

"It depends on who you ask," said Stepan.

Pavel mused, "You give your heart and soul to a cause, but you never get it back!"

"Stop torturing yourself my friend. We'll never understand that war."

Stepan's light handling of the moment reminded Pavel of his errand. He needed to get to the church. Soon he had arrived at Stepan's apartment complex. Stepan's words did not seem to make an impact, and so he added, "you have to uncomplicate your life, my friend. Stay in the present and stay in reality."

6

The Problem of Evil

The small, white-washed study was characteristically Spartan. It had a wall of books on one side and a plain desk, in front of which was a small table and two chairs. The desk was covered with loose papers filled with scribblings, and a Bible. Pavel had just arrived at the church with his family's offering. Father Malashenko was busy talking to the deceased boy's mother, giving Pavel a chance to look over the books in the priest's study. Scanning the volumes, he found scores of books on theology, along with various titles of literature that one would expect in any respectable library. Some surprised him. Glancing past the Russian and Ukrainian literature, he spied additional reads on philosophy, psychology, and a hodgepodge of various other titles, including Nietzsche, Augustine, Jung, and Clausewitz.

The walls were characteristically plain. The only decorative features were an ornate silver cross, and an icon of St. George and the dragon. Painted in egg tempera on linden wood, the icon was as fascinating as it was ethereal. Facing it, Pavel bowed and crossed himself. Leaving the offering, he intended to go, but didn't want to disrespect the priest. He wasn't a regular worshipper at mass and was keenly aware that the priest knew it. Mindful of these facts, he felt more than a little uncomfortable. This was also the first time he'd been in the priest's study.

Just as Pavel thought of excusing himself, Father Malashenko entered with two cups of plum kompot. The aroma of the fruit beverage permeated the small room. Like all Orthodox priests, he wore a long beard that symbolized his dedication to God and had intelligent eyes that squinted from years of intense study. He was gentle, had an easy-going smile that spread across his face, and above all, he had a calmness that Pavel coveted.

"What does it mean to you?" asked Father Malashenko.

"The icon, I mean," he added, clearing his throat.

Pavel furrowed his brow as he thought about it carefully.

"I suppose, the triumph of good over evil," said Pavel, his tone expressing nothing of what he was feeling.

"Yes," said the priest, pausing as if to wonder whether Pavel could elaborate.

"Well," said Pavel, "as legend has it, there was once a village that was terrorized by such a ravenous dragon. To appease the beast, the villagers sacrificed a sheep each day to satiate its hunger. However, they soon ran out of sheep. The king of the land thus decreed that the local children must be sacrificed in order to hold the dragon at bay. Each day, by lot, a child was chosen to satiate the beast. One day, a gallant knight named Sir George arrived at the village just as the king's own beautiful daughter was chosen."

"In righteous indignation, George mounted his noble steed and plunged headlong toward the dragon. Swinging his scaly tail, and thrashing about with his razor-sharp claws, the dragon nearly succeeded in killing George. The knight made several more unsuccessful passes at the beast. In his close encounters with the dragon, managing to parry the stroke of its deadly tail, the knight discovered a vulnerable, scaleless part of the dragon's armor on his chest. Fortified by this discovery, the knight charged headlong into the fray, plunging his lance into the heart of the dragon."

"I'm impressed," remarked the priest.

"As you said," continued Father Malashenko, "the icon represents the triumph of good over evil, and of having the courage to face evil in defense of the innocent."

"Now, my friend, how is your family? How is life?" asked the priest while handing Pavel a cup of kompot. Then, the two of them sat down.

"My family is fine, and I'm okay but I could be better. Thank you, for asking," said Pavel.

"What I'd really like to ask you, Father, I mean, could we take our discussion of George and the dragon a bit further?"

"How so?" asked the priest.

"Well, why does the dragon exist to begin with? Or why does evil exist?"

"You certainly don't ask simple questions," he said while, taking a sip from his cup.

"I'm sorry to have bothered you, Father," said Pavel, intimating that he would leave.

"No, my dear friend. Please stay."

"This is the question mankind asks down through the ages, yet seldom answers. What is evil? Is it bad people doing bad things? Is it a waste of good potential? Or is it good somehow gone wrong?" asked the priest.

"Perhaps, we could put it simply: Evil is the result of following the suggestions of Satan. When we rely on things other than God, we get evil results. Do you see?"

"Yes, a little."

"Encountering calamity causes us to search for answers. Troubles move us to ask how a good God can exist alongside evil."

"Yes, that's certainly true," said Pavel.

"But to answer your question, let me put it another way. In Israel's history, there was once a king named Zimri. He was at one time the servant of King Elah. Zimri's story involves elements of high drama: regicide, a coup, multiple murders, a counter-coup, and then suicide."

"Interesting," said Pavel. "Please go on."

"One day, while King Elah was drinking in his palace, Zimri crashed the party and murdered him, along with every member of the king's family. Believing himself invincible, Zimri then took the throne of Israel. But as it turned out, his fantasy lasted a mere seven days," said the priest as he finished off his beverage.

"In fact," continued the priest, "Zimri went on that week to ingratiate himself in every way, feasting and carousing in lascivious abandonment. Yet, while he gloated in his palace, members of Israel's army learned of his treachery. Incensed, they named Omri their commander and marched against Zimri. Receiving word that the army of Israel had come against him, and was at the very moment outside his gates, Zimri locked himself inside the citadel of his palace. Then, he burned it down upon himself, sweeping away his short, wicked reign in blood and fire!"

"Evil is like this," said Father Malashenko.

"It succeeds only for a season. It rises quickly, dominates for a brief time, but then collapses just as quickly. Evil will not prevail, but good does. The world's evil kingdom will grow, but so will the Kingdom of God."

"But we have such injustice on earth that goes unchecked," replied Pavel.

"Take Andrei Rudenko for example. He worked as a bus driver in Severodonetsk for over fifty years. He received a monthly pension of about 1,400 hryvnias.[1] All I know is he liked his pork chops cut thin. Well, last week, as he was going to wait in line to pick up his check, he caught a bullet in the head."

"Now, I ask you, Father, where is the justice in that?" asked Pavel, raising his hands as he looked up at the ceiling.

"We certainly see injustice, yet God is on the throne of the universe nonetheless."

"My point is, if he hadn't lived in this stinking town, he would have been able to collect his whopping check!"

"I'm sorry you lost your mother. She was a woman of great worth. It was terrible how she died," said Father Malashenko.

"I don't want to talk about her. Not right now."

"Pavel, what I mean to say is this; justice depends on the keeping of promises."

"What do you mean?"

"I mean, God promises to right the wrong. Assuredly, there is a final judgment coming at the end of all time, and yet, sometimes that judgment intrudes into this age."

"I don't understand."

"Well, you may say, 'God makes His rounds.' That is to say, evil will not go unchecked. In fact, we are told that 'evil will slay the wicked.'"

"Do you see?" asked the priest. "This is decidedly the deep end of theology, as well as the so-called Achilles

---

[1] Ukrainian currency: 1400 hryvnias is about $50 USD.

heel of Christianity. As it is said, the presence of evil makes the very existence of God 'problematic.'"

"Okay, but can it be said that a catastrophe was specifically sent by God as judgment for a specific sin?" replied Pavel, almost surprised he was able to articulate the question so well.

"Wow, that's quite a question. Let me say that Scripture does tell us that God sovereignly orchestrates everything on this planet, including natural disasters. And so, nothing falls outside of His sovereignty. Yet, this is not just to say that God simply allows disasters to occur. For we are told in the Book of Lamentations that nothing comes to pass unless the Lord has commanded it. As it is said, 'from the mouth of the Most High woe and well-being proceed.'"

"As you remember, Pavel, this was the essence of what Job said to his wife after he was devastated. His wife advised him to curse God and die. Yet, Job said..."

"Shall we indeed receive good from God and not adversity?" asked Pavel.

"Precisely. My point is this: we may not know why a disaster has come, but we can confidently affirm that the Judge of all the earth will do right. Is that fair?" asked the priest said.

"I want a better answer," replied Pavel.

"That's precisely how Job replied," said the priest.

"The Book of Job deals with two issues crucial to every person: the problem of suffering and the sovereignty of God. In fact, you might say the key question in the Book of Job is: 'Can a man hold on to his faith when things go wrong? Job is fascinating. The whole time Job says all he wants is an audience with the Almighty; 'let me just tell Him my side of the story.' Can you see? Job wants vindication. Then, at the end of it all, the Almighty appears to Job in a whirlwind and Job is speechless. Job then relinquishes his concern to be vindicated."

"Why is that?" asked Pavel.

"Because he believed what he could not fully understand. Do you see? The revelation surpassed reason."

"Job didn't get into the mess he was in because of his own sin. We're told that. However, once Job finds himself in terrible distress, he does not always respond the way he should. And yet, Job argued a good case poorly, while his friends argued a poor case well."

"Here's what I'm saying," said the priest, "the story of Job shatters the myth that living a righteous life can protect one from unjust suffering."

"Can you see? In his suffering, Job comes close to accusing God of injustice. He doesn't quite go that far. And when Job finally gets the audience that he wants with the Almighty, and God finally speaks, does God give Job the answers? No, what God says is, 'where were you when I laid the foundations of the earth? Have you ever designed a snowflake? Did you scatter Orion into the heavens?' And things of that nature. And, at the end of it all, Job doesn't say, now I understand; he says I repent. He doesn't say, 'he repents of the sins that brought the disaster on his head.' Job doesn't need to repent because he is an innocent sufferer; God Himself says so. Rather,

Job repents of the attitude that sought to question God, when Job's horizons of God were so small."

"My point is evil is real. We see its devastating effects all around us. And yet, evil is governed and ruled by God. Do you believe that?"

"I want to believe that," said Pavel.

This really wasn't the answer Pavel was looking for, and Father Malashenko knew it. Pavel believed that he was suffering for his sins, sins he had committed during the war. It was something he wished to discuss. It plagued him. He knew that, eventually, he would have to face the demons of his past, or they would claim him.

An uncomfortable silence ensued. Pavel simply couldn't move himself to talk about the war. Instead, he asked the more indirect question, "Do you think people pay for their wrong-doings in this life?"

"My friend, don't be overly hard on yourself."

"It's a simple question, Father."

"Well, theologically, there is a law of sowing and reaping. The Bible declares that he who sows injustice will reap disaster."

"So, yes," said the priest, "in a manner of speaking, people do pay for their wrong-doings in this life."

Pavel thought, "Perhaps I am plagued by terrible thoughts because of what I did?" Then, he began to think again about that day in Charbagh. He shuddered as a ghost from his past seem to hover over him. He went back to Afghanistan in his mind...

The Soviet column had left Charbagh and was about halfway back to the base. The column reached a stretch of road that channelized to a narrow point with a long adobe wall on one side and a deep, concrete-lined canal on the other. From their elevated position, some two hundred meters above, mujahideen tracked the approach of the Soviet column, then opened fire. Pavel was sitting on a bench seat along with other soldiers in the back of a cargo truck. He was trying to rid his mind of the Afghan boy and those he had buried as the mountainside erupted with machinegun fire – DUH, DUH, DUH, DUH...

Then, a mujahideen warrior fired an RPG. It slammed into the side of the truck's cab – KABOOM! The truck careened off the road, crashing into a rock-strewn gorge, and ended up on its side with its belly perilously exposed to menacing fire. Pavel was knocked unconscious for a few minutes. When he came to, he found the rest of his comrades had scrambled for safety into the gorge. Those not making it were cut down.

In between the burst of machinegun fire, Pavel could hear the familiar Muslim war cry, "Allahu Akbar!" Mujahideen fighters took out the lead and rear trucks, bottling up the column. This left those in between to become sitting ducks. Unable to maneuver, the Soviet commander called in artillery and helicopter support on his own position.

Afghan fighters fired everything in their arsenal. Bullets buzzed and zinged past Pavel's head as he laid as low as he could in the gorge. He watched the overturned truck become a bullet magnet. A 12.7-millimeter heavy machinegun mercilessly raked the Soviet column, gauging holes into the truck's hulk, incinerating Pavel's only cover. Pavel then heard the faint sound of one of his comrades crying for help. "Help. Help. Help me."

Crawling over to the sound of the voice, the bullets seemed to get closer and louder, –THWACK! THWACK! THWACK! THWACK! THWACK! pulverizing the earth all around him. The voice stopped. Then, Pavel recognized one of his comrades, or what was left of him. The bullets got louder and louder. Pavel couldn't seem to get low enough.

"My son, are you ok?" asked Father Malashenko.

Pavel had blanked out for a few minutes, causing the priest to be alarmed.

"Are you ok?" he said again.

"Yes, Father. I'm okay," he said, squinting his eyes.

"Good, I was beginning to worry about you."

As Pavel's mind come back to the present, he sensed he needed to get back to the butcher shop. He thanked Father Malashenko for the plum kompot and the conversation, then he got in his truck and drove away in haste. As his truck turned out of the church courtyard, Pavel glanced in his rearview mirror to see Father Malashenko's hand raised in a benediction.

On the road back to the butcher shop, all he could think about was getting out of Zolote. In his mind, Zolote was now like Afghanistan. In a matter of minutes, Pavel returned to the store to find his father alone.

"Where is Victor?" he asked.

"I sent him on a delivery."

"Okay. Where's the stuff for the trench?"

"Savka took it."

"What? Why?" asked Pavel, pulling nervously at his goatee.

"You were gone for two hours."

"What about Anna?"

"Anna is with Yelizaveta. She's fine."

Pavel shook his head in disbelief. He was speechless.

"I'm sorry, son. You were gone a long time and I needed to deliver some things there before it got too late. Besides, she volunteered!"

"I'll just die if anything happens to her!" thought Pavel.

"Don't worry. All is well," Vasyli reassured his son.

"Go and check on her if you like. I'll close up."

Pavel left in a hurry. As he went, he imagined a host of terrible things that might befall Savka. Fear gripped his mind as he gripped the wheel.

Два

As Vasyli watched Pavel leave in haste, in his peripheral vision he noticed Vano sitting outside the store on a tree stump. Pavel had walked right by him without saying a word. Vano was a thirty-something year old Roma[2] man, to which the Kovals had become *patrons*. Rustling in the back, Vasyli found the items he had laid aside for Vano and his family. Then he picked

---

[2] Another name for gypsy.

them up and walked outside, proud that his family was able to help so many others during these tough times.

"How's Kezia?" asked Vasyli. "And Ehzi? Is that how you say your daughter's name?"

"Yes, sir. She's fine, sir."

"My daughter-in-law has some more clothes for little Ehzi."

"Thank you, sir."

"How about the place you are in? Is it okay?"

"Yes, sir. We are well by God's grace and your goodness, sir," replied Vano.

"Sir, I do not wish to be a burden, sir..."

"It's no burden, Vano," said Vasyli while handing him a bag with some cheese and sausage, and a little bit of bread.

"Thank you, thank you sir. Sir, you are only one I can tell," said Vano, pausing to take a glance around him.

"A policeman took my money."

"Why? What happened?"

"The man asked me where I lived, sir."

"Did you tell him?"

"No, sir," said Vano, shaking his head.

"He wanted to know, but I made something up, sir. But he didn't believe me. Then, he said, 'give me money.'"

"What did you give him? Not all I gave you?" asked Vasyli shaking his head in disbelief.

Vano nodded.

"Dammit! Is there anything more distressing than a corrupt policeman!" exclaimed Vasyli.

"What did he look like? Was he fat?"

"Yes, sir. And then he said, 'around here, Gypsies pay rent.'"

"Rent!" shouted Vasyli.

"That's Yevgan, alright. If that fat slob wasn't hiding behind his badge, and if I was younger..."

"It's okay, sir," said Vano, holding up the bag, "we have everything we need sir."

"Vano, you are good father and husband, if not an unfortunate man."

"Thank you, sir."

"I'm sorry about this. If your predicament doesn't change for the better, then we'll have to figure out how to keep that place you're in warm when the winter comes."

"I once lost my home, too," said Vasyli.

"Really, sir?"

"It was destroyed in the first year of the war. On that terrible day, I lost more than my home. I was here working all day, and I went home not knowing my dear wife had died hours before."

Vano took off his hat and held it in his hand as Vasyli bore his soul.

"It's the problem of evil. Well, I don't want to burden you with my problems, Vano."

"No burden at all, sir. I am deeply indebted to you for all you have done sir."

"Vano, we're going to raise more funds for you. I want you and your family to safely get back to Kherson by the end of this week."

"Give my best to your wife and daughter for me."

Vano then gave Vasyli a deep bow of thanks before walking off.

7

The Trench Line

"Triumph stands in the grasp of the valiant." Such worthy axioms have long invigorated the warrior class since the dawn of time. Ever since the first days of the war, Ukraine welcomed patriotic fighters from other nations. They came in search of glory and triumph. For her part, Ukraine would not deny these volunteers the pleasure. Gathering her own 'foreign legion,' Ukraine could boast of those from as far away as Australia. Made up of various battalions, these soldiers of fortune joined the ranks of Ukraine's Volunteer Army. For their part, the separatists had their share of foreigners, too, the majority being of course Russian, of course, with a sizable complement of Byelorussians and Serbians.

In the vicinity of Zolote, bolstering the defenses on the Ukrainian side of the line of contact, there were several strongpoints which were manned by the Ukrainian Army. Of these strongpoints, some were augmented by the Ukrainian National Guard, which included elements from the volunteer battalions. One of these soldiers of fortune was an American named Thomas Wade.

Thomas Wade was from Richmond County, North Carolina. In the wake of the September 11th attacks, Wade joined the Marines and took part in the invasion of Iraq in 2003. It was the high point of his life. When he came home, he was something of a hometown hero. After his three-year enlistment, he left the Marines, and took odd jobs in the Carolinas.

At a commanding position, east of Zolote 4, sat an army strongpoint, known to the soldiers as strongpoint two. From this dugout position, the terrain sloped down to the Komyshuvakha River to the east. To the south, on the other side of the train tracks, could be seen the woodline and the stacks of Pervomais'k's coal mines on the distant horizon.

"Wade," called out a Ukrainian sergeant.

"Here."

"We have a new recruit. He's a Spaniard, another unpaid volunteer. His Russian is pretty good, perhaps better than yours. Give him an overview of where we are in the war."

"That'll keep me here longer than my shift," complained Wade.

"That's okay. He's assigned to your squad. Take him with you."

After the sergeant left, Wade said under his breath, "You'd better leave. I'll knock you so hard," he said, nursing a grudge, "you'll see tomorrow, today."

"See tomorrow, today?" asked the Spaniard, a little confused. "Now, that's a very interesting concept."

"Ah, forget him," spat Wade. "That guy couldn't find his butt with both hands and his back pockets."

The Spaniard cocked his head to one side with a puzzling look.

"Forget it," said Wade. "Now, let's get down to business."

"Sit here, friend." Wade grabbed an ammo crate and set it before him.

"Thank you," he said.

The man walked down the wooden steps into the trench. Detecting what smelled like feet and dirt, he brushed the dirt off the crate and sat down. The area he sat in was shaped much like a narrow inground pool, lined with logs and sandbags. The floor consisted of wooden planks. From where he sat, the trench line narrowed until it was about six feet wide. Winding around larger trees, along the edge of a field, it ran on as far as his eyes could see. Laying his AK-47 across his lap, the man took a cigarette out of his jacket and lit it. He took several drags, then looked at Wade.

"Okay, I see they gave you a helmet, a rifle, body armor, and a load-bearing vest," mumbled Wade.

"How many magazines have you got?" quizzed Wade.

"Five."

"Okay, that'll work. So, why are you here, friend?" asked Wade.

The man looked shocked to hear such a question.

"Well, I want to stop the separatists and the Russians, of course."

"Friend, its 2019. It's now the fifth year of the war. If you're here to stop the Russians, then I'm afraid you're too late. It seems that they're here to stay."

"I see your point," replied the man.

"But if your desire is to sit in this trench and get yourself killed, then you've come to the right place," added another soldier.

"That's Ivan," said Wade, "and as our esteemed sergeant announced earlier, I'm Wade."

"Just Wade?" questioned the man.

"My name is Thomas Wade, but everyone just calls me Wade."

"Now, what's your name, friend?" asked Wade.

"My name is Alonso Moreno. I'm from Sevilla."

"Ah, Sevilla! Lush boulevards, tantalizing food, and, of course, bullfights! As it is said, there are the two curses of Spain, the bulls and the priests," declared Wade.

A youthful thirty, Alonso was characteristically the quintessential Spaniard. He had a stubble beard and wore his hair short-cropped, which he combed to one side.

"Let me guess, you had nothing better to do? Or are you an idealist? Perhaps you're a modern-day Robert Jordan? But then again, that wouldn't work," mused Wade, "you're not a communist."

"I'm a patriot," said Alonso proudly. "My fight is against tyranny, wherever it prospers."

Wade let out a wide smile. "My, my, you are indeed an idealist."

"What did you do for a job?"

"I taught high school history."

"A historian? Well, I'm supposed to give you an overview of where we are in this war, but I reckon you could do a better job. What do you say? Let's start with what you know. What would you say happened here?" Wade prompted.

"Well, from what I've heard, it all started with protests against President Yanukovych, and his decision to keep Ukraine out of the European Union. This, in turn, sparked protests centered at the Maidan square. Matters soon escalated, prompting him to flee."

Wade sat quietly and slowly rubbed the stubble on his chin. "Go on."

"Then, in March 2014, Russian troops captured the Crimea, and later annexed it under the pretense of protecting Russian citizens."

"Have I got it right?" asked Alonso.

"Well, butter my butt and call me a biscuit!" exclaimed Wade.

"What?" asked Alonso, puzzled.

"What about here? How did this mess start?" inquired Wade.

"Oh yes, I was just getting to that," replied Alonso.

"Within two months of Russia annexing the Crimea, pro-Russian separatists here in the Donetsk and Luhansk regions declared independence from Ukraine."

"Let's see," Alonso went on, "and since that time, a lot has happened. Who can forget about the Malaysian Airlines flight the separatist shot down? Or the battle for Donetsk airport? Or the separatists downning the Ukrainian transport?"

"Well, my friend," said Wade, "seems you have quite a grasp of what is going on here. They should put you in charge," he said jokingly.

"But what you may not know is where the war is going or how it will end... and neither do I, and I suspect neither does anyone else. But what I do know is they make a big deal here about language. You could say it's the fuel for the fire."

"When I got here," continued Wade, "I could barely speak any Russian. And when the subject of the Ukrainian language versus the Russian language came up, I didn't realize the difference. At first, to me they sounded the same. But what I've found is, they're more like Spanish and Italian. To make matters more confusing, some even speak a mix they call Surzhyk. But something I realize that I don't think they do is, that language itself does not equal identity."

"What do you mean?" asked Alonso.

"Well, you and I are here in this trench, talking about life matters in Russian, a language that's not our mother tongue."

"You and I are speaking Russian, but that doesn't make us Russians."

"I see," said Alonso.

"So, here's my two cents," said Wade. "This war is all about identity. What do you think, Ivan?"

"What I think," said Ivan, "is that things have gotten a little livelier around here."

"Really?" Alonso asked.

"From what we know, last night, some separatists jumped over that part of the trench line," informed Ivan, pointing in the direction of Partyzansky.

"Really? Isn't there a minefield out in front?" asked Alonso, staring at the space in Ivan's tooth.

"Yeah."

"Then, how did they make it through?" probed Alonso.

"Beats me. But that's sure keeping Captain Volokh up at night," rebutted Ivan.

"Who is Captain Voloo-kuh," enunciated Alonso, having trouble with the pronunciation.

"VOL-LACH," rectified Wade. "Well, he's the commander of this section of the trench, and you'll meet Lieutenant Testenkov later, he's our platoon commander. And you already met my 'friend' Sergeant Kravets. Those three make things happen around here."

"What about the separatists that made it through this position? What of them?" pressed Alonso.

"All I know is that there was quite a ruckus. I was in the barracks, taking a meal, when all of the sudden, all hell broke loose somewhere over there," said Wade, pointing north of the trench line. "There was, as they say, a FIREFIGHT!"

"Alonso, have you ever been in a firefight?" inquired Ivan.

"No, I haven't."

"Don't worry, there will be one here soon enough," said Wade, sardonically.

"Besides, everyone always pisses themselves the first time, don't they Ivan?" teased Wade, giving Alonso an encouraging nod.

"Who shot at them?" asked Alonso. "The army?"

"No, it was a militia."

"There's still a militia here?" Alonso asked.

"Well, it wasn't us, so it had to be militia," said Ivan.

"It was a militia, and a rather short fight too. Like a knife fight in a phone booth, it was over quickly. And from what I hear, they got 'em good. The field quickly became hell's half-acre!" exclaimed Wade.

"So, you see Alonso, despite what Ivan says, there's never a dull moment around here. This sort of thing happens all the time."

"It's the Kremlin's secret little war," added Ivan.

"Perhaps, the best overview of what's going on here is this," said Wade, "the rebels want the people of Zolote to equate any death in their town with our presence. Their logic is simple: cause us to fire into the cities, then the people will flock to their pro-Russian banner."

As Wade began to explain trench life to Alonso, the sobering sound of incoming mortar shells could be heard whistling their way toward their position.

"Hit the deck!" yelled Wade, grabbing Alonso and throwing both into the bottom of the trench. Within seconds, three mortar rounds fell in succession. They cracked and whooshed, throwing shrapnel fragments and dirt skyward.

WHOOOOOOP! WHOOOOOOP! WHOOOOOOP!

"Ah! You can hear the Minsk peace agreement!" yelled Wade.

Sending sheets of dirt down on them, the three rounds impacted about a hundred meters in front of their position. Then, a phone rang. Wade picked up the landline handset.

"This is four, go ahead."

"Four, this is six. What's your status?" pestered Lieutenant Testenkov.

Standing up to brush himself off, Wade responded, "Six, we are a hundred percent. The others watched their sectors and then glanced back at Wade.

"Yes... okay... yes sir... we'll keep our heads down," said Wade, with a smirk as he hung up.

"When does the lieutenant come out?" asked Alonso.

"Not often," Ivan said thankfully, with a smile.

"Which is no problem," said Bogdan with a hint of sarcasm in his voice, sarcastically.

"As you can tell, our lieutenant is not exactly popular. Let's just say, he's a far cry from Misha, our last platoon commander," said Wade.

"Now, that was a great leader," said Bogdan.

"Alonso, this bear of a man with the grenade launcher is Bogdan," introduced Wade.

Bogdan gave Alonso a firm handshake. "Misha kept us alive last winter. He always knew what to do. And if he didn't, he'd ask," said Bogdan.

"Yes, a real man's man," said Ivan.

"Perhaps we'll have time to tell you about him; that is, if we survive the day," said Wade, cynically.

The pungent smell of the explosive residue filled the trench. New to the sensation, Alonso commented, "It tastes like dirt and metal."

Seconds later, the fields in front of their position erupted with a staccato of gunfire, followed up by several RPGs – TUUUPHHH... TUUUPHHH... BOOOOM! BOOOOM!

It was a familiar ploy of the rebels, trying to goad them into fighting.

"Get down! Spread out!" yelled Wade.

Two more RPGs exploded – BOOOOM! BOOOOM! The rockets hit a tree, sending branches, dirt, and leaves flying.

"Return fire!" roared Wade. Then, picking up a walk-about radio, "Bravo, this is Alpha. Get out here!"

The radio squelched, "Moving."

Ivan, who had been near the PKM, mounted it. He laid down a long, cyclic base of fire, nearly going through the whole drum – DUH, DUH, DUH, DUH, DUH, DUH, DUH, DUH... The others mounted the trench wall, joining the fray – B-B-B-BRRAAAAAAW!

"Sustained rate," barked Wade, wanting Ivan to lower his rate of fire.

On the opposite trench, muzzle flashes could be seen through the camouflage netting. Wade called for Bogdan to bring up his AK-47 with attached grenade launcher. "Fire that thing! Just watch the branches!"

Leveling his rifle at about a forty-five-degree angle, Bogdan fired the grenade. It made a burping sound – WHOOOFP! followed by a thudded BOOOM!

"That oughta fry their balls!" yelled Wade, as he smiled.

The landline radio began to ring again.

"Look at us," Wade said to Alonso, "a hundred years later, and we're back to fighting in trenches!"

Wade picked up the landline handset again.

"This is four, go ahead... Yes, give me a minute."

"Alright, who's dead? Everyone still alive? Great!"

Wade picked up the landline., "Yes, sir. We're at a hundred percent."

The shooting continued sporadically for several more minutes before dying, then died down. Wade and the others were hesitant to stand up. As soldiers often do, they simply took the opportunity to take a break right where they were.

Still mounting the PKM, Ivan sat the butt of his machine gun on the ground, leaned up against the trench wall, and lit a cigarette.

"Friend," said Alonso, "since we are getting to know each other, may I ask you a question?"

"Fire away," said Wade.

"What brought you here?"

"Well, let's just say, it's a cause I believe in."

Everyone laughed.

"No, really?" pressed Alonso.

"It was either join the French Foreign Legion or come here to fight tyranny."

"That's fair," responded Alonso.

"Would you look at that!" remarked Wade.

Half covered in dirt, nonetheless, one could still make out the Soviet star. Wade walked over and pulled it free from a freshly blasted part of the trench, revealing a warped and shrunken leather belt. Then, he held it up, turning the belt's face toward Alonso.

"A World War II Red Army belt," declared Alonso. "I would venture to guess, it held up the pants of a Red Army soldier who no doubt marched through these parts in the summer of 1943."

"Go on," said Wade, who loved history.

"Well, from what I recall," said Alonso, sitting back down on the ammo crate, "the German Sixth Army had just been annihilated at Stalingrad, then it reconstructed itself as best it could as it fell back to this region here. As the Nazis dug in, the Red Army came at them with over a thousand tanks, and a million men. Within a week, the Red Army drove the Germans back to Donetsk. And our comrade here, well, he didn't make it as far as Donetsk."

"Maybe he died of boredom," joked Ivan.

Wade carefully broke off the caked-on dirt to reveal a near-flawless artifact. Then, he pulled up his digitized multi-cam jacket and held the rustic Soviet belt buckle next to his own. It was roughly the same size.

"A CSA belt," said Alonso. "Where did you get it?"

"It's somewhat of a family heirloom, you might say," said Wade, as he sat down on an ammo crate.

Wade took off his helmet and scratched his head. He could sense the others wanted to know.

"Alright," he said, "But pull security while I talk. Let's get ourselves ready for the next gunfight. Check your mags, bring that drum of ammo to the PKM," instructed Wade, as the men checked their weapons.

Wade went on. "This belt buckle was once worn by my great-great-grandfather, William Thomas Wade. He was the First Sergeant of F Company, 44th North Carolina Infantry Regiment, known as the Trojan Regulars."

"Oh my God!" exclaimed Wade. "Those bastards killed our supper!"

One of the mortar rounds had scored a direct hit – on Wade's soup experiment.

"Do you have any idea how long it takes to boil potatoes!?" screamed Wade, directing his voice to those across the trench line.

Ivan picked up a piece of potato off the floor of the trench and ate it, "It just needed another ten minutes."

"Well, since we're not having potatoes," said Wade, "give me one of those smokes, and I'll finish my story."

Ivan gave him a cigarette and lit it.

Wade took a long drag and went on, "He joined up in April of 1862, and right away they went into action at Tranter's Creek. Burnside's 24th Massachusetts tried to push inland. They held them there before heading, then they went north to join Lee's Army of Northern Virginia."

"During the American Revolution?" asked Ivan.

"American Civil War," corrected Wade. "Anyway, when he missed Gettysburg, the 44th was left to guard rail lines. But, as it turned out, he most likely would have been cut down in Pickett's charge. When Lee came back into Virginia, well, that's when the real fun started. For the next two years, my great-great grandpappy slugged it out with the Federals in something like twenty or so engagements: Bristoe Station, the Overland Campaign, Spotsylvania Court House, and Cold Harbor. After that, the Siege of Petersburg is where they met up with old Burnside again – to live in trenches like these."

"After Petersburg, they just keep moving west. Then, Lee surrendered at Appomattox. And after he was paroled with the others, they took his guns and sent him home. It was April 9, 1865, Palm Sunday. His shoes were plum wore out. For the next four days, he walked home in those worn-out soles to Richmond County, a full two hundred miles. It snowed on him as he passed through Pittsboro. Then, he reached Rockingham on Good Friday, and heard the news the next day that Lincoln had been shot... Civil wars are the most uncivil of all wars. Anyway, this is the belt he wore."

"What did he do when he got home?" asked Ivan, dropping his cigarette, putting it out with his boot.

"He did the same thing every veteran does, he got married and had kids," he said as he laughed.

"I never heard that story before," said Danylo, who had run out of the barracks to the trench line.

"Me neither. Just when I thought I had heard all your crazy stories," remarked Oleksandr.

"Danylo, Oleksandr, meet Alonso," said Wade.

"Hello, sirs," said Alonso.

"You know what's funny, Wade?" led Ivan.

"No, what's that?"

"Shouldn't you be on the other side of this trench?"

"What do you mean, friend?"

"Well, you're a rebel!" joked Ivan.

"Hah-hah, very funny... there is an American fighting for the other side. He's a tool who plays a guitar. I think his name is Charles Nolan; he's a Texan communist!"

"Really? Now, I've heard it all!" exclaimed Alonso.

"He's a steer and a queer!" jested Ivan.

"No, that's Oklahoma!" replied Wade.

Alonso leaned up against a tree and lit a cigarette. "Who were those people who checked my rifle's serial number?"

"What?" asked Bogdan.

"He means the OSCE," said Ivan.

"The OSCE," said Wade, explaining the acronym: Organization for Security and Co-operation in Europe. They're supposedly the ones ensuring there's a cease fire."

They all laughed.

"Sure, there's a cease-fire during the day," said Oleksandr, "and when the OSCE go home for the night, well, that's when the real fireworks begin."

"You see, officially, there are no Russians here. The Russian media parrots this narrative. You know, you invade, and then say you didn't. It's brilliant!" said Danylo.

"I know one of them, an OSCE monitoring officer, that is," said Ivan.

"Her name is Yvette, I think. A beautiful Dutch girl."

"Oh, you dirty dog," teased Wade, slapping his shoulder, prompting a round of laughter.

"I saw her last month when her team came down here. It was the day Oleh got it."

"Yeah, Oleh sure could play," said Bogdan, strumming an imaginary guitar.

"But what does she look like?" asked Wade.

"Well, she's a Dutch girl. You know, tall, blonde and beautiful."

Alonso tried not to stare at Ivan's teeth as he talked. They were distracting. He had a space about the width of a tooth between his bottom incisors. One of them was even canted and raised itself unaesthetically above the others.

"How's her veneers?" asked Alonso, "I mean, does she have a face like the girl in Vermeer's painting?" asked Alonso, trying to recover from his Freudian slip.

"I'm not sure. I'll have to find out."

"What do you mean? You don't remember what she looks like?" asked Wade.

"No, I mean I don't know who the hell is this Veneers girl," said Ivan.

They all laughed, relieving some of the built-up tension they had from the firefight.

"To answer your question Alonso, they're watchers," said Wade.

"They watch the line of contact," added Oleksandr.

"They also hand out food. So, I guess they're pretty much like the UN," said Ivan.

"Well, now that we're all here," said Wade, "this brings our squad up to six men. There's you, me, Bogdan, Oleksandr, Ivan, and Danylo," listed Wade, as each man in turn raised his arm. They were a motley crew, all brought together by the circumstance of war.

"We're all volunteers assigned to the 92nd Mechanized Brigade. There are three squads to our platoon, and as you can see, things here are really pretty simple."

As Wade began again to explain to Alonso the daily scope of life in the trench to Alonso, Savka arrived. She stood at the entrance to the trench where the town met the woods. She was a good fifty meters away, yet, she was close enough to gain and maintain Wade's undivided attention. He closed the distance, taking a long hard look at her as he did. Then, before he got too close, he said to Alonso under his breath, "She's as fine as a frog hair split four ways; even with that crazy blue hair."

Savka placed the basket down and laid out the contents of food and drink.

"Thank you, ma'am," said Wade, with a wide smile.

Savka broke into a smile, which sent a jolt of electric current down Wade's spine. He found it increasingly difficult to avoid looking at her. Her brown hair was dyed blue and tumbled over her shoulders. She had a photogenic face, black eye makeup, a nose ring, full hips, and a pair of Amazonian legs. As Wade took in the view, a goose waddled over to Savka, squeaking and honking at the unknown guest.

"You've met Masha," said Wade.

"She's our goose. She lives over there," said Ivan, pointing to a little barn the soldiers had built for her.

"Awe, what a sweetheart," said Savka stroking her head, causing Masha to honk playfully.

"How did she get here?"

"I'm not sure. She was here last summer when I got here," said Wade.

"I was told she had some goslings when this place was just a field," he added.

"You're American?" asked Savka.

"How'd you guess?" answered Wade, sarcastically.

"Where are her babies?" asked Savka, as she looked around.

"Apparently, her goslings are gone, but she sticks around," said Wade.

"Ah. That's so sad," replied Savka.

"Yes, but we take care of her. You could say, she's our mascot," said Ivan.

"We have a cat too," added Wade.

"Yeah, we're becoming a small zoo!" joked Bogdan.

"Don't mention the cat," said Ivan, with a traumatized expression on his face.

"Hah, Sasha is a black cat. Ivan doesn't approve of her," said Wade.

"I don't approve. Cats are bad luck," said Ivan.

"Ivan believes a cat can sense trouble before it happens," said Wade.

"Is that true?" asked Savka.

"It's most certainly true," said Ivan. "She was here laying in the sun until a few minutes before this last attack. Then, she sniffed the air and ran off."

"But she likes you, Ivan," said Bogdan.

"No. She doesn't! Don't put that hex on me," Ivan snapped.

"As you can see, Ivan is very superstitious. He even believes cats can tell when someone is going to die," said Wade.

"They can," said Ivan, in a solemn tone.

"Ivan, I think you and my mother share the same brain," said Savka.

Just as things were getting interesting for Wade, Pavel arrived. "I heard shelling. Savka, are you okay?"

"I'm fine."

"It's not safe here!" said Pavel.

"True. We just got hit," said Wade.

"Soldiers," said Pavel, with a slight bow of his head, "thank you for your loyal and patriotic service to our country."

"Please accept these items as a token of our gratitude," he said, pointing to the basket of sausages, bread, and cheese.

"Our pleasure, sir," said Wade, as he shot a smile at Savka. She smiled back.

"Please visit anytime you like," said Wade like a lovesick schoolboy.

Wade watched her as she walked away. He had long entertained the notion that if a woman liked you, and was walking away, she'd glance back at least once. He wasn't disappointed. As she drove off, Wade said, "God created woman, and at that moment, boredom ceased to exist."

8

Sector Command

Of all the things most disconcerting, loss is perhaps the greatest. Recovering the package was therefore the one thing motivating Vadim. It was Tuesday morning, and a sector command meeting had been called. It was supposed to happen on Wednesday, but the sector commander, Oleg Rudenko, was concerned about the firefight Sunday night. He therefore called for an earlier meeting.

Using the back roads to avoid army checkpoints, the black sedan carrying Vadim, and two others, drove east out of Severodonetsk and into the farmlands. Observing the load signal, which was two sheets hanging on a clothesline, one blue and one white, Dimitri sped down the country road toward the farm. The road led out of the woods into a field, which looked like it hadn't been plowed in over five years. Reaching the end of the road, they arrived at a large building on the edge of the woods. It was an ancient Cossack barn, painted white with a thatched roof.

Arriving inside, the three were greeted by Oleg, a former Ukrainian officer. His ideological leanings were Russian. Like many others, when the war came, he gravitated to the separatist cause. The barn had been hastily cleared of straw, albeit the pungent smell of cow manure lingered. Inside the barn, a single table and several chairs were dwarfed by the massive walls of the old structure. On the plastered wall, opposite the door, was a map of the Donbas. Red marker demarcated the boundaries of *Sector Karbonit,* which encompassed the land immediately north of the line of separation, running north up to Severodonetsk, west toward Popasna, and then east toward Kryakivka.

Of the twelve separatist sectors, *Karbonit* was perhaps the most organized. On the map, various colored pushpins indicated places of significance, including Ukrainian Army bases and various checkpoints, and strongpoints along the trench line. Oleg glanced at his watch, it was 10:00 am.

"Gentlemen," he said greeting everyone, "thanks for your pains in making this meeting a reality. We have pressing matters to attend to. I will now ask Partisan

Commander Vrilnik to brief us on the current enemy situation."

"Thank you, sir. Comrades, as of 0800 hours this morning, our intelligence has confirmed that Ukrainian military forces haven't made any significant changes in their dispositions. The 92nd Mechanized Brigade is currently at ninety-percent strength."

Vrilnik could boast of about a hundred fighters, armed mostly with AK-47s. Some of them had older weapons, including bolt-action rifles or even pistols. For the most part, his men were like Mosby's partisans. His men lived and worked in the surrounding towns and villages, but could be called up within about a half hour for a major operation, and then melt back into the landscape.

"As I'm sure you've heard, on Sunday night some eight of our men were ambushed as they crossed the contact line, just west of Partyzansky. Let's just say things didn't go so well."

"That's quite an understatement," said Oleg.

Vadim eyed Oleg loathingly. It grated against his narcissistic sensibilities, that he should have to answer to a man he believed far beneath him in every way. For his part, Vadim would play the game, masquerading as a true team player on Oleg's team.

"They went early. They were supposed to wait for nightfall," said Vadim.

"Yes, but it wasn't the army that hit them," said Vrilnik.

"Where did this militia come from? I thought the militias were disbanded?" asked Oleg.

"I could chastise the man who's at fault, only, he has already paid with his life for his mistake, having died in the ambush," said Vadim, ignoring the question.

"Further," added Vrilnik, "we have just learned that the police have detained one of our men from that party. He's being treated for his wounds at the hospital in Hirske. OSCE agents have identified him as Alexei Petrov."

"However, three managed to get through. They brought us our rockets," said Dimitri, in an attempt to find a silver lining.

"With the acquisition of the RPGs, the mission wasn't a total failure barring the loss of men," said Vrilnik, gaining a low murmur of approval.

"Well, Vadim," said Oleg, "in light of this setback, do you feel we are still safe to proceed with the plan?"

"Is anything in war ever safe?" replied Vadim, gaining a few laughs.

"Nothing about this plan is safe," said Vadim, "but I think the plan is salvageable."

"As the partisan commander has stated, the army hasn't added any more troops to their strongpoints," he said, anticipating the question.

"So, the enemy just got lucky, eh?" questioned Oleg.
  Vadim nodded.

"Comrades, as you know, our eventual goal is to push the contact line back, so as to create a new line that will bring all of Zolote within the LPR sphere," Oleg said in a rousing tone that gained a cheer.

"Gentlemen, it is time," he added.

"Now, in order to make this happen, our mission will be first to open a gap in the line at Zolote 4. This will gain a foothold for the LPR's Phantom Battalion to flow through. How I intend for us to do just that is a raid on the army strong point at Partyzansky at Zolote 4," he said, indicating on the map.

"This will be executed by partisan commander Marko and Colonel Kerlikowski's LPR combined force of thirty-five men. They will be staged at Kobalt Mine number three. Under the line of contact here," he said, pointing to a place on the map in between Kobalt mines three and four.

"Vadim's team has dug a mineshaft that's approximately two hundred meters long, connecting the two pre-war mines. The total distance underground is nearly four-hundred meters."

"The shaft is ready, yes?" asked Marko.

"Just finished it yesterday. We had to pump a lot of water out of it," said Vadim.

"Only, don't light a match down there," quipped Dimitri.

"When you pump out the water," he explained, "it pushes up methane gas."

"Just have it ready, and my men will do the rest," said the LPR commander, Colonel Kerlikowski.

"What about response times from the Ukrainian Army?" asked Marko.

"We can expect that they will not move in force, for fear of triggering the massed Russian troops across the border," said Dimitri.

"Since the drawback, the largest Ukrainian concentration is just east of Popasna; the 92nd Mechanized Brigade. Response time is estimated to be twenty minutes. Once the shooting starts, they'll most certainly use this road," he said, standing up to indicate the road between Popasna and Zolote.

"That's where you come in, Vrilnik," said Oleg. "You will lay an ambush just east of Popasna, to cut them down as they race to rescue their strongpoints. At the strongpoint, Marko and Colonel Kerlikowski's men will only be facing a few squads of about twelve to fifteen men. Their attack will be supported by our very own guest FSB[1] sniper," said Oleg, as Gorgan raised his arm.

Colonel Kerlikowski stood up. "Once we knock out this stretch of trench line, we will move at once to take control of the city administrative building located here."

As Kerlikowski went on, this aspect of the plan reminded Vadim of the siege of Odessa in the early days of the war. In the wake of Euromaidan, clashes between pro and anti-Maidan groups broke out in Odessa in May of 2014. The anti-Maidan group wore orange and black striped ribbons of St George on their clothing, identifying themselves as pro-Russian. Reports told of both sides being well-armed. The clashes culminated in a large street brawl outside the Trade Unions House in downtown Odessa.

Losing ground, the pro-Russian group retreated into the Trade Unions House, only to be firebombed with

---

[1] Russian Federal Security Service (FSB). Successors of the KGB.

Molotov cocktails, while others fired pistols and rifles into the windows. It all ended in blood and fire. Forty-two separatists were burned alive, suffocated, or jumped to their deaths. Among them was Vadim's only son, Andriy. It seemed to Vadim that Oleg's plan would follow a similar trajectory, ending in disaster.

"Comrades, once we've taken the city council building, I will call for the remainder of my battalion to push forward," said Colonel Kerlikowski with a bow.

"My friends, this is the moment we've been waiting for. By Saturday afternoon, all Zolote will be under our control. Then, we'll be staged for the next big push to Kharkiv!" clamored Oleg, as those in the barn stood up to cheer.

"We'll move into position Friday at 1800 hours. Any questions?" asked Oleg.

As the meeting concluded, Vadim stood up to leave. He had no sooner reached the door when he was met by Fyodor Chornyi. Fyodor had been a member of the Druzhina's auxiliary for about a year, helping the circle in various ways. Like many, he joined the separatist cause through Vkontakte or VK.[2] Banned by Kyiv in 2017, it had quickly become the preferred social network platform of the separatists.

"What do you have for us today?" asked Vadim.

"Something I know you'll like," said Fyodor.

"Really?" asked Dimitri.

"Go on," said Vadim.

---

[2] A type of Russian Facebook.

"His name is Victor Nimchuk," he said, with a hint of regret.

"That seemed hard to say. Is he a friend?" asked Vadim.

"No," he said, shaking his head.

"A mere acquaintance. But an enemy nonetheless."

"How is he an enemy?" asked Vadim.

"Another miner like Taras?" asked Dimitri.

"He's not a miner. He's a butcher...."

"Okay, let's meet and discuss it later," interjected Dimitri.

Vadim's cell buzzed in his pocket. He read the text, "I HAVE THE MONEY. LET'S TALK – YEVGAN."

"MEET ME AT KOBALT TWO TOMORROW AT NOON. COME ALONE," replied Vadim.

Vadim and Dimitri walked over to the black sedan to find Gorgan standing there.

"Whatever we do from here on out, let's not trust one of them. That plan will never work," said Dimitri.

"You're probably right," said Vadim.

"We have to get a hold of that money!" said Gorgan.

"Patience, my friend," said Vadim.

The three men got into the car.

"When the dust settles, we'll have a bigger piece of the pie," said Vadim.

"What about the money?" asked Dimitri.

"It seems we'll need to talk to our lecherous little police chief about that," said Vadim.

"And?" asked Gorgan.

"We'll get it," said Vadim.

"What about Oleg and his cronies?" asked Dimitri.

"What of them? The sheep smear sheep! They say 'comrade' and speak of Novorossiya as though it will be part of the USSR 2.0," said Vadim.

"That's a laugh," added Dimitri.

"My friends, the secret of reaping the greatest fruitfulness and enjoyment in life," said Vadim, "is to live dangerously. I have a plan within their plan."

"I'm all ears," said Gorgan.

Два

The walkabout radio squelched, "Bravo, this is Alpha... Bravo, this is Alpha."

"Go ahead Alpha," answered Ivan, picking up the walkabout.

"When you come out, bring water."

"Roger, Alpha."

Ivan set down the radio and walked back to the table. "It's July! If you're going out to the trench, bring some frickin water!" snarked Ivan.

Wade, Alonso, and Ivan were on a break in their barracks room. It was a commandeered apartment complex that was in close proximity to the trench line. Shared by the Army and the volunteer battalions, each floor had its own ecosystem. The volunteers occupied the ground floor, using only a few apartments for living quarters, and the army had the rest. On the second floor, the army set up a make-shift tactical operations center or TAC. On the ground floor, one of the rooms was converted into a break area for the soldiers.

While the apartment was too close for comfort for civilians, it was perfectly situated for those fighting in the trench. Three of Wade's men were out on the strongpoint, while he and two others were killing time playing a new game called rummy. Wade had introduced the game the day before.

"Where were you off to yesterday?" asked Wade, shuffling the cards for another hand.

"Me?" responded Alonso.

"Yes."

"Why do you ask?"

"Just curious friend."

"What's her name?" interjected Ivan, smiling from ear to ear. He then went on to catalog a long list of women's names. When he came to the name 'Zlata,' Ivan discovered a tell, and so did Wade.

"You don't have a very good poker face," said Ivan.

"He sure doesn't."

"I went with a guy in another squad. It's a place just up the road."

"Friend, Hirske is not just up the road. It's nearly three kilometers."

"So, you've discovered 'the Wolf's Lair?' Nice place, huh? Good music, ladies..." said Ivan alluringly, as he shook his torso.

Alonso was becoming red in the face.

"I didn't know it was a brothel," he whispered.

"A brothel!" laughed Ivan.

"Relax friend. I'm not making a judgment call, we're just not supposed to be that far away, at least not without a pass."

Wade looked at Alonso. He was blushing bright red.

"Leave him alone Ivan," said Wade, trying to lighten things up.

"Okay, so let's see..." said Ivan, trying to remember the rules of the game.

"No friend, you have to discard," said Wade, explaining the rules of the game.

"What?"

"Just put down a card you don't want."

Wade sat his cards face down on the table and took a sip from his coffee.

"You sure like that coffee," said Ivan.

"I do, but why on earth it hasn't ever caught on here is beyond me. You guys and that tea."

"No. No. No. That's not a set," said Wade. "You have to have a set. You know, six, seven, eight of spades, or three of a kind... You guys invented the game, didn't you?"

"Alonso, since you're a history professor..."

"Teacher," corrected Alonso.

"Okay teacher, and since Ivan can't play this game, maybe you could tell us about his people?" asked Wade, motioning to Ivan.

"What's your last name?" asked Alonso.

"My last name is Kulak," responded Ivan. My father Andrei Kulak, survived his little sabbatical in Archangel, then he returned here to the Donbas."

It was rapidly becoming something of a game for the men of the squad to quiz the Spaniard on history. Alonso sat down his cards and lit a cigarette.

"What was his name before it was Kulak?" asked Alonso.

"He knows so much!" said Ivan. "It was Rudchenko."

"Rudchenko, eh? Ah, the terrible class struggle!" exclaimed Alonso.

"To achieve his enormous feat of industrialization," said Alonso, breaking out in a diatribe, "to have enough food, and 'to give each according to his ability, from each according to his need,' Stalin had to modernize the agricultural system of the Soviet Union."

"You mean, he had to steal land in order to make huge farms," said Wade, sarcastically.

"Precisely. You see, in his mind, he would make the farms larger, and therefore, more productive. But who wants to give up their land, especially when they're not compensated?" asked Alonso, rhetorically.

"Well, the farmers or 'Kulaks' were not compensated," Alonso elaborated, "and yet they were expected to work with other farmers and hand over everything they owned to the government. I would venture to guess, because your father refused this scheme, this 'collectivization,' he was evicted from his land, and sent to a labor camp in Siberia."

"Yes," said Ivan.

"And knowing that most Kulaks were worked to death, I'd say your father was a rather strong man to come back here alive. Have I got it right?" asked Alonso.

"You have!" exclaimed Ivan. "All but the part about my mother."

"My father met her in Kharkiv when he returned."

"Well, I must say, I'm impressed friend. You certainly know your history."

"The question is, what will you write about us in years to come?" asked Ivan.

"Perhaps," said Alonso. "Anyone can write a book."

"When you pin your treatise on this Russian imperialism, remember, we Ukrainians are free farmers and warriors! Unlike the Russian slogan of total rule, ours is 'God, freedom, family, and the motherland,'" said Ivan, with a bow.

"I'll be sure to," replied Alonso.

"Okay, so a rooster sits on a roof top. It lays an egg. Which side of the roof does it roll down?" asked Wade.

"The right? No, the left. I don't know," said Ivan.

"Neither. Roosters don't lay eggs," said Alonso.

Wade laughed and glanced at his wristwatch. "Time to rotate."

"Let's go," he said as he put on his jacket and kitted up. Wade had one standing order: Leave the building ready to fight to the death. Within minutes, as he had done hundreds of times before, Wade relieved the soldiers in the trench. He was soon back in his familiar place, looking out at the field, with the slagheaps, and the industrial chimneys of the factories in Pervomais'k off on the horizon.

"Peace on earth, we sing it. Then we pay a thousand priests to bring it. But after two thousand years of mass, we've got as far as poison gas."

"What's that, Wade?" asked Ivan.

"Just an old poem. Can't remember who wrote it, but he sure was right."

"I've been meaning to ask you," said Alonso, "what do we do if we get overrun?"

"Overrun?"

"If things get that bad, run like hell, out of the trench, and to the city council building. We'll do our best to link up with the militia there, then circle the wagons until the cavalry arrives."

Wade then went on to tell Alonso all about the militia and Lev, their leader. "All told, they have about twenty or so fighters. If we can, we'll also link up with them."

As the hours wore on, the monotony of trench life set in. As all soldiers know, there's nothing quite as menial as a guard shift. Wade brought his coffee out with him. He rested it on a familiar log and passed the time taking sips. Masha waddled up to give him company.

"Silly goose. I didn't forget you," he said, grabbing a bowl out of his cargo pocket and setting it in down. He filled it with water and fed Masha some cabbage he had carried out of the barracks.

As a veteran, he knew daydreaming was dangerous. It was only midday, and all Wade could think about was Savka. Despite his earlier pontificating to Alonso, he had decided that as soon as it was dark, he would go see her.

Три

It was Tuesday afternoon, Vadim, Dimitri, and Gorgan returned from the sector command, and arrived back at the mine office to find the assembled circle. Everyone could sense that Vadim was a bit irritable. The first order of business for him was to formulate a plan to get the money back. The question on his mind was, what to do about the meddlesome police chief?

"What do you propose?" asked Dimitri.

"An ambush," said Vadim.

"How?" asked Gorgan.

"I need for him to feel safe. I want him to arrive feeling he has the upper hand," replied Vadim.

"Where is the meet?" asked Mr. Green.

"Kobalt 2 mine at noon tomorrow," said Dimitri.

Vadim sat pensively, smoking a cigar. "I've got it," he said, letting out a sinister grin.

"We'll have the meet in the parking lot, and you can set up in an abandoned office," he said to Gorgan. "Does that work?"

"That works."

"Ok. There's another aspect to this. The chief has Alexei. He took him this morning," said Mr. Red.

"What do you mean?" asked Dimitri.

"I mean he took him under guard. I don't know where. I'm assuming to his office," said Mr. Red.

"This changes nothing," said Vadim, as he stubbed out his cigar in an ashtray. "He already has the money."

"Shouldn't we inform Oleg?" asked Father Mitka.

"No. This is our business," said Vadim.

"Ok. We have a plan," he said, visually checking in with the others. "Alright. Now you can let him in."

The door opened and Fyodor joined the meeting.

"Now, my young friend, where were we?" asked Dimitri.

Fyodor pulled out a chair from under the table and sat down. Vadim held out a box of cigars.

"No, thank you. Well, like I was saying earlier, he's not a miner; he's a butcher. So, I talked to this guy yesterday; a nobody in the mine, and he starts talking about the ambush that went down Sunday night. He says that he heard Victor Nimchuk talking about how he and some others in a militia attacked some 'ORDLO thugs.'"[3]

"Really? He said that?" asked Dimitri.

"Yes. He told everybody. He wouldn't shut up. I wasn't sure until he told me too."

"You're right. This is something I really like. I'd like to talk to this Victor right away," said Vadim.

"I know where he lives," said Fyodor.

"How do you want to do it?" asked Dimitri.

"Let's do what we did last year in Hirske with the journalist. Maybe use your new man. What's his name?" asked Vadim.

"Anatoli."

"Great. Have the young Anatoli brought in."

---

[3] Occupied Regions of Donetsk and Luhansk Oblasts.

Четыре

It was now Tuesday night. Reviving a long-standing custom, Pavel took his wife out for dinner. He wanted to spend a quiet meal with her and discuss moving. At around 7:00 pm, they arrived at the *Bell Ringer*; a charming family-owned restaurant in Hirske. It was a happy place where customers could become friends with the staff and the owners, who were Nina and Petro Ponomarenko. In the years before the war, Pavel and Yelizaveta frequented the place. For them, the restaurant seemed like a home away from home. And though they hadn't been away for quite some time, upon entering, they sensed a sort of homecoming.

The tantalizing smells of country cuisine met them as they walked in the front door. After a warm greeting, a waitress seated them in a quiet corner, a welcomed sight after being so long on his feet. Pavel sat as he normally did, with his back to the wall. He recognized the comfortable view of the entrance to his front, the kitchen to his left, and every table visible to his periphery. Pavel carefully scanned the clientele scattered about. There were perhaps ten.

"I talked with my sister today," said Pavel.

"What do you know... new menus!" said Yelizaveta, as a blonde waitress approached their table.

"Hello Oksana!" said Yelizaveta. "I'm so glad you're working tonight!"

"Hello! How are things?" asked Oksana.

"Things are going well," said Yelizaveta, with all the cheerfulness she could muster.

Oksana was respectfully attentive as Yelizaveta gave her a rundown of her life to the present. While he zoned out, Pavel began looking around the room. A long stucco wall opposite the kitchen was made up of built-in shelves, holding an assortment of pottery and jars of fruit. The rustic old wooden tables were covered with rushnyk cloths, giving the place a traditional look and feel. Oksana lit the candle on their table, filled their glasses with water, then took their order: Golden crisp deruni for her, and caramelized onions atop varenyky for him.

"You said you talked to your sister. What did you and Laryssa talk about?" asked Yelizaveta.

"You know… a job… where we'd live, things like that," said Pavel.

"And?" she prodded.

"I'm still trying to figure it out," said Pavel, clearing his throat.

"I've got to go to the bathroom," said Yelizaveta.

"Okay," he said, anticipating a fight.

"Perhaps the night will be a total loss," he thought.

No sooner had she gotten up, that suddenly a man dressed as a waiter walked over and sat down at their table. Pavel's look was one of surprise and annoyance.

"Are you lost?" asked Pavel.

"Your father is in grave danger" he said.

"What are you talking about?"

"There's a separatist group operating clandestinely within these border towns. They have an extensive network. They're keeping tabs on people and have been watching your father's activities."

"Activities? What activities? Why are you telling me this?" asked Pavel.

"You really have no idea what is going on, do you? They know about your father," said the man.

"They know what?" asked Pavel, watching Yelizaveta walk back to the table. The man stood up.

"Tell your father to lay low for a bit," said the man as he stood up.

"Your food should be out shortly sir," said the man, refilling Pavel's glass. He then walked away.

After the man left, Pavel hardly said a word to his wife. The two of them quietly finished their dinner and then went home.

9

The Vanishing

Evil, it is said, is done naturally without much effort. It may be argued that metaphysical evil gives rise to physical evil, which in turn brings to pass moral evil. And the amount of evil transpiring in Zolote was becoming difficult to keep up with.

There were numerous abandoned buildings around for Gorgan to choose from. Reading the terrain and the environmentals, he decided to set-up in one overlooking the parking lot of Kobalt Two. In an abandoned third-floor factory office, he took up a position deep in the room. Then, with ritual care, as he had done hundreds of times before, he took a tripod out of his bag and elongated it, affixed his rifle to the tripod mount, loaded five rounds, then he set the data on his scope, sighting in his target area. The whole procedure took less than a minute. His position afforded him an easy two-hundred-meter shot for his .338 Lapua. He then scanned the parking lot through an opened window on the other side of the room. Then his eyes came to a stop at a point near the entrance. Satisfied, he waited silently. It was now a few minutes past noon on Wednesday and it began to rain. The rain created a soothing sound as each drop resonated on the tin roof of the abandoned factory. Pouring through a hole in the roof, the rain began to fall in a cascade in the middle of the floor.

Yevgan arrived. He was alone and drove into the parking lot. He parked his car about a hundred meters from where Vadim stood out in front of his black sedan. Stepping out of his car, he was dressed in his camouflage police uniform. He was about fifty years old and somewhat portly. Closing the car door, he walked toward Vadim. Carrying a bag in one hand, he cleared a pistol from under his jacket and leveled it on his nemesis.

"My dear police officer, I'm only a businessman. I'm here to negotiate," said Vadim cordially.

"Where are your employees?"

"I gave them the day off."

"You've been here now… a year, is it? And in that time, how many bodies? Thirty… forty?"

"Who's keeping track," said Vadim callously.

"My soul has," replied Yevgan.

"I should have arrested you long ago."

"But business has been good for you nonetheless?"

"Yes, but this time, I want more than just a payoff," said Yevgan, gritting his teeth.

In a long, pregnant moment, the two men stood motionless, staring each other down, while the rain pummeled the ground around them.

Vadim broke the silence. "After standing on the sidelines for so long, are you now prepared to choose a side? What did you have in mind? And would you mind lowering your weapon?"

"There are a lot of questions being asked around here about bodies. So-and-so's father never came home; so-and-so's son is missing. The last one was a boy!" yelled Yevgan.

"The worm that's fled hath nature that in time will venom breed."

"You don't scare me," said Yevgan, as the rain pelted off his soaked form.

"Where's Alexei?" asked Vadim.

"He died. Didn't you hear?"

"How did he die?"

"Am I a doctor? How should I know? He just bled out in the hospital."

"Did I call you? You called me! Now, what do you have for me?" asked Vadim.

"I should kill you now. It would be the only righteous death we've seen around here lately."

"Go ahead... But if you do, you'll never have half of the company."

"This company? Kobalt?" asked Yevgan, lowering his pistol. He squinted his eyes and wiped the rain off his face as he thought about the proposal. Another long moment passed, then he said, "Done."

Vadim smiled, then took several side steps, moving to the left-front corner of his car. Cocking his head, Yevgan watched Vadim with an amused expression, laughing as he found himself framed in Gorgan's crosshairs. A second later, a shot rang out, echoing the distinctive report of a high-caliber precision rifle. Yevgan fell to his knees, breathing out a deep gasp. Looking down, a long spatter of blood poured out of his mouth. The bullet had ripped through his upper chest, just below his right collar bone.

Gasping for air, he looked up at Vadim, and tried to raise his arm to get a shot, but then fired a round in the rain-soaked dirt a few feet in front of him. With his life force having left him, he fell like a sack of cement, face first in a puddle. Vadim walked over and grabbed the bag; inside was a plastic wrapped rectangular block of one-hundred dollar bills, a half-million still intact.

"I don't scare you, huh?" asked Vadim.
Vadim cleared a pistol from under his shirt and fired a round into the back of Yevgan's head. A moment later, Yevgan's naked body was left alone in the parking lot.

Два

One of Pavel's great skills was presenting a false face to others. Planning to wear this mask all day, Pavel worked in the back of the butcher shop, scarcely showing his face at the counter. Surprisingly, Victor was also quiet, making things twice as good for Pavel. Working alone always cleared his head. Besides, he had already decided to leave early the next day for Odessa. As the day wore on, circumstances allowed him to avoid his father. After all, he didn't know quite how to tell his father he was leaving. As soon as it might appear as though Vasyli would get a minute to engage with him, another customer would show up to his rescue. This was okay with Pavel, who was rather content to go about his business working in the back. His conscience stung him. Was his father in trouble? But then he dismissed the idea entirely.

"The mysterious man had me confused for someone else. Today I'll go home and, tell Tatyana and Savka," he thought.

"After all, Tatyana doesn't really like her job anyway, and Savka can find a new life. They'll understand," he told himself. He needed only to get home and pack some things. "I'll find work," he thought, "I'll labor especially hard to make things work out."

"Besides," he thought, "what's at the apartment that we can't replace? We could just leave without it all."

Before long, it was five o'clock; time to go home. In a rush, he washed his hands, hung up his apron, and flew out of the door to the truck. It all took a few minutes. He wisped by Victor and Vasyli and had just shut the door of his truck when his father walked out of the shop in haste to say goodbye for the day. Pavel lowered his window as he backed up, "goodbye," he said. "See you later."

The thought of finally leaving the Donbas caused his mind to course with new ideas. He was ecstatic and enraptured with all the new possibilities. "Ah, Odessa and the sea. I'll finally put this stinking town in my rearview mirror," he said as he grinned.

The two-minute drive home was over in seconds. With a newfound zeal, he seemed to hurdle the steps up to his apartment in one continuous leap. As he broke the threshold of the apartment, he was met by Yelizaveta. She was upset. Her hair was disheveled. She had been crying. She handed him a note, then sat back down on the couch, putting her hands over face, and shaking her head. As if telepathically, Pavel knew it was about Savka. He unfolded the letter and read the following:

Father,

It's with great distress that I write to you. I overheard you and mom talk about leaving. Let me say in short, I have found love again. I won't leave. I simply can't. I am alive again, and I won't leave. Don't worry about Anna and I. We'll be fine. Please understand, and please don't try to find us. I know we'll see each other again one day. Don't worry. I'm sorry, as I know this will hurt you both. Please forgive me.

Love Savka

As he read the letter, each word hit him hard. The longer he read, the deeper the words cut into him, until he felt like a wild animal trying to free itself from a trap. Pavel finished reading the letter aloud and handed it back to his wife before entering, then walked into the kitchen.

"What the hell! That's just great! Now what am I going to do?" he yelled, slamming his fist on the countertop. Then, he sat at the dining room table, and let his palms fall on the table with a thud.

"Where are my daughters?" he yelled, banging his hands on the table.

"She could have at least told us where she was going!" Then, with a violent sweeping motion, he swept everything off the table onto to the floor – "AAHHHHH!"

He got up and walked into the living room and sat down in his high-back chair.

"Did you tell her?" he asked, looking at his wife.

"No, I didn't!" replied Yelizaveta, upset at the question.

"Why would I do that?" she said, getting up to pick up the shattered pieces of the vase, amongst the other things on the floor.

"What about Tatyana?" he asked.

"I didn't tell her either!"

"Okay, okay, just let me think!" he said.

"What could she be thinking?" he said as he walked into Savka's room. "All her things are still here."

"She just took some of Anna's clothes," said Yelizaveta, tearing up at the mention of her granddaughter's name.

"I'm sorry, my love," said Pavel, as he sat down next to his wife and consoled her.

"If we live through this, someday we'll be happy again, I swear!"

When Tatyana came home from work, the apartment reeled again in renewed anguish. For Pavel, it was his dark night of the soul.

Три

Victor parked his car. He had just driven home from work and began to walk to the door of his apartment block. Nearing the door, he heard the screeching of tires. He spun around in time to watch a car careen off the road and slam into a parked car.

"That's my car!" yelled Victor, as he jumped with its impact. The jarring sound echoed within the quad of the buildings.

"What the hell!" he yelled, as he ran over. "What the hell are you on?"

A young man in a brown leather jacket stumbled out of his wrecked Opal, bending over holding his neck. "Ah, my neck!"

The car that imploded into his was an old banger. Victor cursed as he walked over.

"I'm so sorry," said the young man.

"Sorry is right!" exclaimed Victor, confident that he could whip the other man.

"What we're you thinking? We're you driving fast enough? Did you mean to take up this same parking place as my car?!"

"I'm so sorry. I'm sorry. I'll take care of this!"

"I know you will," said Victor, becoming increasingly irate.

"Friend," said the young man, "let me offer you some money."

"What do you mean?"

"I don't want to get the police involved."

"Why not?"

"I don't have insurance."

"What?"

"Or a license."

"AUGH!" said Victor, shaking his head.

"I'm sorry."

"Enough of being sorry!"

"I will make this right. Look, your car isn't damaged that bad. Look at mine."

The front of the young man's Opal was totaled. While Victor was yelling, a steady stream of smoke was pluming out of the banger's radiator, which was now somewhere near the glove compartment.

"What do you have in mind?" asked Victor.

"Drive me to my house."

"What?"

"No, really, it's just down the road a bit... in Stakhanovets," said the young man.

"Then what?"

"I'll give you five thousand ruples."

Victor looked at his car. It wasn't banged up that bad. Besides, he could use the extra money.

"Okay" he said reluctantly. "But help me get your wreck off my car."

Victor got in his car and backed up. Pushing the young man's car to the other side of the parking lot. Then he rolled down his window. "Alright. Get in."

Четыре

That night, Pavel had a terrible dream. One he had dreamed many times before. He was back in Afghanistan, on the airbase in Kabul. It was night, and the dead and wounded were still being hauled in from another attack, an all too frequent event. Mujahideen fighters had ambushed another unit as it was returning to base.

For the next few hours, the base swarmed with activity, like a busy ant hill. Then, after a few hours, things began to quiet down. Soon, all that could be heard were the muffled groans of the wounded. Then, in the dead of night, all hell broke loose. The base rocked with explosions. Balls of fire plumed high into the cold night sky. Grabbing his rifle and falling out of his tent, Pavel rubbed the sleep from his eyes. Stumbling over to his assigned position, he barely managed to put on his flak vest, boots, and helmet. Out in front of him, in the cold blue and purple tones of the moonlit no man's land, were hundreds of jihadis pouring over the perimeter. Their eyes were aglow with the allurements of the celestial bliss awaiting them.

Raising his AK, Pavel took careful aim at a mujahideen fighter that was closing on him. He pulled the trigger, but his weapon wouldn't fire. He racked the bolt again and again, but nothing. At a charge, the holy warrior bellowed out a terrible cry of "Allahu Akbar!"

Just as he was right on top of Pavel, another comrade's rifle blasted away, dropping the jihadi to the ground. Throwing down his AK, Pavel picked up the felled warrior's rifle. Wheeling around at the sound of another war cry, he took aim and took the slack out of the trigger, but the weapon failed to fire. Pavel cursed the weapon, and just as the fighter was close enough to spit on him, bullets from another man ripped through the charging Afghan, throwing him to the ground. Pavel watched him flail wildly in the thralls of death, raising his hands as if to heaven, his fingers bent and curled, as his soul left his body.

Instinctively, he dropped the magazine to check if it was loaded; it was. He cursed again. Looking down, he saw that his clothes were covered in blood. In a panic, he dropped the rifle and began patting himself. He discovered the blood wasn't his own. The next second, he was punched in the jaw by an Afghan warrior. Swinging wildly, the Afghan connected several hard blows to Pavel's head, sending him to the ground. The fighter jumped on his back, pummeling him further. Covering his head with his arms, Pavel yelled as the mujahideen warrior landed punch after punch. Pavel felt that at any moment he would black out.

BOOM! An RPG exploded, throwing him high into the air. He was so high, he felt as though he were freefalling thousands of feet. Then he landed face first with a thud. He stood up to find himself in a ditch full of bodies. The stench of decaying flesh was overpowering. Somehow, the dead had freed themselves from the covering dirt. The ghoulish remains of the disembodied howled, crying out for vengeance. Hearing the voice of a lad, Pavel whirled around, seeing the boy wearing the green kameez. Only it wasn't shiny anymore, but stained and mildewed, covered with maggots. The boy still clutched his side, dragging his entrails as he walked about the ditch. Out of his mouth poured a torrent of blood and maggots. He suddenly awoke, "Oh God! Oh God!" Raising himself, he sat up on the edge of his bed.

"It's okay! It's okay," said Yelizaveta, reassuringly. His face was deathly pale, as grave as a man being led to his execution. His heart was beating out of his chest. He sat there for a long while, feeling as though he was losing his mind. Then he threw on his shoes, ran out of the bedroom, and sat down in his chair. Yelizaveta came out to console him, but he would have none of it.

"Why won't you let me help you?" she insisted, her eyes full of emotion. "You never let me help you!"

Pavel sat silently.

"You don't need to wear a mask with me," she said, frustratingly.

"Please don't drink again," she said, as tears began to fall down her cheeks.

"Leave me alone," he said. She soon relented and went back to bed. Pavel then began to think about Boryslav Popov.

"He was always in such high spirits," he thought.

"He could make you laugh even if you were dying."

"As it turns out," thought Pavel, "you found life just as dark and depressing as I do. I guess the war finally claimed you, my friend. As I suppose it will with all of us."

An hour later, he found himself in his chair with his only friend, a bottle. The next hour, he found himself on the roof of the apartment complex, standing on the corner, on the precipice of the unknown. He raised the bottle, knocked it back, then threw it out into the night. He could hear the bottle burst as it found the road.

Standing on the edge of the roof, he looked out into the night sky at the vast sea of stars. Suddenly, a thought came to him.

"Oh Stepan, you old rascal," he said as he bellowed out a great laugh. "Your philosophy has helped me out at last!" he said as he stepped down off the ledge.

"He who has a *why* to live, can bear almost any *how*."

10

The Interrogation

"Is it true," said Vadim, "that to live is to suffer, and to survive is to find some meaning in the suffering?"

The delirium was wearing off. Victor awoke to find himself in an office, seated with his arms and legs taped tightly to a wooden chair. He squinted his eyes, recovering consciousness.

"You must be full of questions," said Vadim, as he looked out of the window at the gathering rain clouds.

Jagged bolts of lightning flashed across the sky, reverberating off the surrounding hills.

"Is your name Victor Nimchuk?" interrogated Vadim. Victor confirmed his name with a shrug.

"Who are you?" asked Victor.

"Who I am is of no account. But what I want to know should interest you – immensely."

Vadim took out a cigar and lit it.

"Let's just say your friend sold you out."

"Who?" asked Victor.

"I will ask the questions."

Vadim pulled up a chair and positioned it close to Victor.

"Now, I'm going to ask you some questions. You should answer as truthfully as you can. Okay?"

"Okay," said Victor nervously.

"You are a member of the militia, are you not?" demanded Vadim. "Are you a member of the militia?" he repeated.

Victor sat paralyzed with fear.

"My young friend, the West is decadent and Zelensky is a clown. Did you know that? Every militia you raise, I will bring down."

"Who brought you into the militia?" he snarled.

"I know you're a part of the militia. Just give me a name and perhaps things can go well for you" said Vadim, setting his cigar on an ashtray, then taking a pair of pliers in hand.

"Now, let me share with you a technique I perfected in Syria. I believe it will amaze you," said Vadim, savoring the pleasure of the moment.

Beads of sweat began to run down Victor's face. Placing his left hand over Victor's right hand, Vadim took the pliers and squeezed firmly down on the nail of Victor's little finger.

Frozen in terror, the color drained out of Victor's face.

"Now, I'm going to ask you again, who brought you into the militia?"

Victor said nothing. In one slow and steady motion, with his cigar clamped between his teeth, Vadim pulled the nail until it separated from the nail bed.

Victor howled in horror – "AHHHHHHHH!"

A dark stream of crimson flowed forth like molten lava as he tore the nail free from Victor's digit. Vadim's devilish work exposed the sensitive flesh under the nail. Setting down the pliers, Vadim took several long pulls of smoke, and then, squinting his eyes, he held the fiery ember of his cigar about an inch from the traumatized digit.

"No. No. No!" Victor cried out in agony.

"Who brought you into the militia?!" thundered Vadim.

Victor closed his eyes and shook his head, causing Vadim to smile savagely. He hovered his cigar for another second, then lowered it, making contact. The exposed raw flesh sizzled, causing Victor's body to heave in pain.

Picking up the pliers, he placed them near Victor's hand as though he would continue.

"Who brought you...?"

"Vasyli!" blurted out Victor, gritting his teeth in anguish.

"Vasyli? Vasyli who?"

"Vasyli Koval.... the butcher."

Vadim slowly nodded his head as if to say, I knew it all along.

"You know, I once did this to a man for three days in Chechnya. He was a real tough bastard; a mujahideen holy warrior."

"But you," he said, shaking his head, "I'm not so sure about."

Victor looked around at the room he was in. It seemed as though he was at the mine office, but he wasn't sure.

"You recognize this room? You should. You used to work in this mine, before you started working for THEM."

"They're all clowns. You'll see. This is my world, not yours!" said Vadim, baring his teeth.

"Now, you answered that question well enough. But what I really want to know is, where were you Sunday night?"

Victor stared back in defiance.

"You heard what I said."

Victor could hear the door open behind him. Then, the young man from the parking lot stood in front of him. The last thing Victor remembered was walking into his apartment. Carrying in a bottle of vodka, he sat it down on the table and winked at Victor.

Victor erupted, "You sack of cow dung! I'll kill you!"

"You know something? torturing people always makes me thirsty. Are you thirsty?"

Vadim set down his cigar and poured himself a glass of vodka. He took a drink. Then he poured himself another glass, purposefully spilling some on Victor's wounded finger, launching him into a spasm of pain –

"AHHHHHHHH!"

"You know, the aim of torture is not to make someone talk per se, but rather it's to destroy the person as a human being, to destroy a person's identity and soul."

A rush of fury gripped Victor. With all his might, he strained to wrest himself out of the chair.

"Now, that's the spirit," said Vadim, watching Victor spend himself in a feeble attempt to get free.

"You can do it!" said Vadim.

"AGGGHHH – the devil take your soul!" yelled Victor.

"He already has."

"Don't you believe in God? You can't be this evil and get away with it."

Vadim laughed. His eyes burned with a demonic force.

"Haven't you lived here long enough to know that God isn't here? He isn't anywhere. He doesn't exist!"

"Besides, I find it hard to believe in a God who wants to be praised all the time."

"Who are you?"

"We are the Trojan Horse."

"Now, my young friend, where were you Sunday night?"

Victor closed his eyes again and shook his head from side to side. Then, taking the pliers in hand, in one rapid movement, Vadim jerked the nail off Victor's ring finger, causing him to scream out again in horror –

"AHHHHHH!"

"He passed out," said Dimitri, who had been sitting behind Victor the whole time, "but he'll talk. They always do."

"You did well, my young friend," said Vadim, gently slapping his face.

"Anatoli, is it?" asked Vadim, turning to the young man who had brought him the bottle.

"Yes, sir."

"Well, Anatoli, as you can see, one must never underestimate the power of the human spirit."

"It's a shame we have to break him. It really is. He would have made a fine addition to our little group. Too bad he's been corrupted."

"I suppose, it would have taken a lot more than that to draw what I needed out of him," said Vadim with a sigh.

"You know, Dimitri, after coming into contact with a religious man, I always feel that I must wash my hands."

Два

It was Thursday morning, and the new month of August had begun. Pavel was looking forward to making his midweek trip over to the church. It would serve to take his mind off his life, which he felt was in shambles. He would deliver his family's offering and have a chance to talk again with Father Malashenko. Since solving the problem of evil had become too illusory for him, he'd settle for solving the problem of satisfaction.

When he arrived, he found Victor's mother Katerina out in the church courtyard talking to Father

Malashenko. Pavel was still in his truck as they glanced over.

"Victor!" he thought, "I had forgotten all about him! He never came to work. He had vanished."

"Vanished!" he thought. His mind suddenly raced with terrible thoughts about Savka and Anna.

"My dear sweet little Anna," he thought.

"No, I can't and won't think about you right now. Not right now," he told himself.

Nonetheless, he went there in his mind. He suddenly thought about the time Savka ran away. She was barely sixteen and disappeared for nearly three weeks. He gripped the wheel in anger as he remembered those anxiety-filled days and sleepless nights.

"How on earth will I get through this?" he thought. Shaking off the doldrums of these unpleasant thoughts, he got out of the truck and walked over as Katerina was leaving. He bowed respectfully as he passed her, then gave his greetings to Father Malashenko. "Good afternoon, Father."

"Good afternoon, my son. Will you come inside? I have just made tea."

"I can't," said Pavel, not wanting to intrude, but wanting to stay and clear his soul, nonetheless.

Father Malashenko took the basket of goods, "then, just for a few minutes?"

"Okay."

Before they reached the priest's study, Pavel asked him, "We still don't know where Victor is, do we?"

"No. And I suspect something terrible has happened."

"I do too."

"But what about you? How are things with you?" asked the priest, showing genuine concern.

"I feel as though the life that I'm living is a search for meaning."

"Oh," said the priest with a smile, "well those two go hand in hand. Do you see?"

"No. But I'd like to understand," said Pavel as he stepped into the priest's study.

"Well, in a sense," said the priest, "we're all on the same journey, searching for meaning. Many just go about it the wrong way."

Father Malashenko could sense Pavel was not in quite as big of a hurry as he made it. He poured him a cup of tea, and the two of them sat down. Then, he watched Pavel glance around the room, stopping to look again at the icon of St. George and the dragon.

"Perhaps I could put it this way. At the risk of sounding rather sermonic, may I share a thought with you from the sobering Book of Ecclesiastes? It's from a passage I was reading this morning."

"Please do."

"It's a thought I've dwelled on a lot lately. Solomon tells us about those who take the route of wisdom, believing that wisdom alone will bring them satisfaction."

"I see," said Pavel.

"But then, Solomon says, apart from God, such a quest will lead only to despair."

"Why is that?" asked Pavel.

"Well, it's because the wisdom we can acquire is merely from under the sun. Do you see?" asked the priest.

"No, I don't."

"It's because mere earthly wisdom, as amazing as it can be, will not supply meaning or lasting satisfaction. And because wisdom's route doesn't work, Solomon goes on to say that many invest themselves in pleasure."

"Well, I certainly remember that about Solomon," said Pavel, "What was it... three hundred wives and seven hundred concubines?"

"Yes. Yet his point is, the God who made us, did not make us to be 'satisfiable' by the mere pursuit of pleasure. I'm sorry, I didn't mean to preach."

"No, Father, really, it's okay. My soul needs this."

"My point is, meaning and satisfaction have to come from someplace outside of this life, from Someone above this life. That is the wisdom of Solomon. And so, man's search for meaning is meaningless apart from God."

Pavel was struck by the simplicity and solemnity of the priest's little homily.

Три

The buzzing sound of a low-flying drone could be heard as it whooshed overhead. Wade ran out into the trench.

"Was it ours?"

"Not sure," said Ivan. "But if it comes over here again, it's getting blasted."

Drones had long been used by both sides for reconnaissance and surveillance. The OSCE also used them for monitoring purposes, but as to whose it was, wasn't altogether clear. The rebels also used them to drop grenades. Seeing one, therefore, got everyone's attention.

Finding a comfortable spot, Wade rested himself against the edge of the trench. He scanned the field out in front of him with his rifle scope. Glancing off in the distance, Wade noted the familiar stacks of Pervomais'k's coal mines. A single trail ran from the woodline on the other side of the field to his position. He could clearly make out the field, up to about six hundred meters. The train tracks split the field in half. On the friendly side of the tracks, along the trail, the Army had placed several dragons' teeth to ward off tanks.

Scanning his sector, he saw Sasha. Her black fur glistened in the afternoon sunlight. Wade saw her coming from the ORDLO[1] side and wondered how the food she got over there compared with what she received

---

[1] Occupied Regions of Donetsk and Luhansk Oblasts.

on the Ukraine side. She sauntered down the trail over to where Ivan was and sat down, not a meter from his head. She was there several minutes before Ivan turned his head at the sound of her purring.

"Shoo! Shoo!" yelled Ivan.

"Ah, you're too superstitious," said Wade.

"Okay, you guys come over here and I'll tell you what we have to worry about next," said Wade.

"Now what?" asked Ivan.

"You remember that last contact we had?"

"Yeah."

"Well, the next strongpoint over, the one near Orikhove..."

"Yeah."

"Well, they got hit so hard that the ORDLO managed to get some guys in the trench. By the time they took it back, one of their guys was missing."

"Really? Well, I guess they wanted payback for Mozgovoy," said Ivan.

"No. Mozgovoy died in 2015," said Wade.

"Was he captured?" asked Alonso.

"No, an elevator was rigged with an explosive device, blew him into eternity."

While Wade went on to discuss the SBU's cross-border raids and assassinations, the thud and crack of 82millimetermortars shook the ground in front of them – "THUD – CRACK, THUD – CRACK, THUD – CRACK."

The warheads impacted a mere fifty meters in front of their position. Everyone immediately threw themselves at the wall of the trench. Another three rounds fell in succession – "THUD – CRACK, THUD – CRACK, THUD – CRACK."

"Stay down," yelled Wade.

The sudden mortar attack was followed by an eerie silence. Then the landline rang, and Wade picked up the receiver. "This is four... yes, sir... yes, sir. Okay out," said Wade, as he dropped the handset.

"Here, give me that bullhorn," said Wade, and in a display of great chutzpah, he held his cellphone's speaker next to the bullhorn and began to play the Ukrainian national anthem: *"Ukraine has not yet perished, nor its glory and freedom... Fate will smile on us once more... Our enemies will die, as the dew does in the sunshine... and we, too, we'll live happily in our land... souls and bodies we'll lay down all for our freedom... and we'll show that we, brothers, are the Cossack nation!"*

As the anthem played, the squad swelled with pride. Then, came the familiar crack of incoming bullets, the tracers tearing into the trees above them. The frequency increased to an all-out enfilade. Volleys of machine-gun fire chewed up the dirt right in front of Wade, nearly taking off his upheld arm.

"Whoa! Thank God for sandbags," yelled Ivan.

"Yeah," said Wade, "the more you have, the longer you live."

"Anyway, keep a buddy near you. You don't want to end up like that other poor bastard."

The two sides traded rounds, and the landline rang again.

"I'll get it this time," said Ivan.

"Okay," said Wade.

Then after a few minutes, things began to taper off to an uneasy silence.

"Well gents, you've never really lived until you've almost died," said Wade, grinning.

"I've been meaning to ask you, Wade," said Ivan.

"Yeah, what's that?" he said, scanning his sector.

"Is America ever going to get more involved here?" he added.

"Well, as Alonso could tell you, ever since the Bolsheviks won, America has always fought the Bear by proxy, as in Korea, Vietnam, Afghanistan, etc."

"I guess what I meant to ask is, will Trump continue to help us?"

"Well, I believe he has, to the tune of hundreds of millions." said Wade.

"All I know is it's been a crazy year so far: An actor beat himself up while saying some Klansmen in MAGA hats attacked him, the Venezuelan people are starving under another dictator, Notre Dame Cathedral burned down, Robert Mueller's report found nothing, and Hong Kong is on fire."

"They say Russia intervened with US elections, and that Hillary lost because of it. Is that true?" asked Ivan.

"Yeah right! More like Russia intervened with US media," said Wade, with a smirk.

"My friend, Russian efforts to influence the American media didn't start in 2016," said Alonso.

"Huh, that's an understatement! But what good are the opinions of thousands, if none of them know anything about the subject?" asked Wade, rhetorically.

"What do you mean?" wondered Alonso.

"I mean people are extremely gullible. They see two talking heads on CNN and believe whatever they hear. It's all fake news!" added Wade. "They invent new words in an attempt to create a new reality!"

"Let me put it like this. Back in the 1980s, we had the WWF, that is, the World Wrestling Federation. You might have heard of it. Yeah... no? Okay, anyway," continued Wade, "everybody knew it was fake; we all knew it was fake. In fact, if you were to ask anyone back then, they would all say it was fake. But the WWF people pretended like it wasn't. The funny thing was, everybody knew it was fake, but watched it anyway. Later, the WWF people admitted that it was fake, and that it was just for entertainment. And so, the question is, when will the mainstream media admit the same thing?"

"Provocateurs and opportunists," said Wade, thumbing his hand on a sandbag.

"If we survive the day," said Wade, "I'll tell you more about what I think America is going to do here. But let it be said that, truly, the media is the hired hand of a monied system. It has no other purpose but to tell lies when its interests are threatened."

Wade glanced at his watch, finding his mind again on Savka. Soon his shift would be over, and so would his torment.

11

The Butcher Shop

For a butcher shop, it was first rate. Proudly serving the people of Zolote for over eighty years, its first owner was aptly named Artem Reznik. A kind-hearted soul, he took a liking to Vasyli. And perhaps longing to save him from what he believed would be certain death in the mines, he hired him on as an apprentice. Artem often joked that it would take a full year for the last of the coal dust to be washed off Vasyli. In one sense, the coal dust never left him. After he became the sole proprietor, Vasyli renamed the shop *The Meat Hook*. It was situated a good distance from the frontline, and so managed to remain unscathed, and continued to be busy.

The building itself had a pleasant seat, conveniently situated along the main thoroughfare running from Hirske to Pervomais'k. Due to its position on the road, it was something of a community center, where one could not only find fresh meat, but also catch up on the latest news and gossip.

Upon entering, the first thing one encountered was the long glass coolers encasing a wide assortment of meats. Like most butchers, Vasyli placed his meats in rows. From left to right: first were the sirloins of lamb, then the chops, next, the beef in a similar fashion, followed by poultry, and last, the pork. As Vasyli would often jest, "meats should be arranged according to their level of nobility."

To the sides, the shelves that lined the walls were filled with various canned goods; among the most popular were borscht mixes, and jams. Hanging above the glass displays were hams and other smoked meats; these were brined and proudly smoked in-house. Capping the whole establishment, as with most places of business in Ukraine, there was a place of honor for various icons mounted on the walls above the shelves, along with the gold and sky-blue Ukrainian flag.

Pavel had just returned from visiting Father Malashenko. He now hoped that the last hour or so of work would distract him and clear his head. Upon entering the shop, Pavel found his father looking rather piqued.

"Pavel, would you mind taking over for the rest of the day? I feel I'm coming down with a cold," said Vasyli.

Knowing he would have the rest of the day to himself, he dutifully acquiesced. "Sure father. Summer colds are the worst!"

"How is Father Malashenko?" asked Vasyli.

"He is well, and thanked us for the offering."

Vasyli soon left, and Pavel found himself alone again with his thoughts. As the day wore on, he encountered the store's afternoon clientele. First, there was Galina. Pavel couldn't recall her last name. She picked up her customary two pounds of pork loin. She was followed by Nina and Petro Ponomarenko, owners of *The Bell Ringer*. They virtually cleaned out all that was left of the chicken and ground beef.

"How's business been? And where's your father? Is he ok?" asked Petro.

"He's fine; just a little tired. I guess that happens when you get to be his age."

"Yes," he said, and as he turned to leave, Petro saw Victor's mother walk in.

"Old age is the only thing that comes to us without effort," he added.

"Hello Mrs. Nimchuk," said Pavel, with all the solemnity he could muster.

"Hello," she said meekly.

Pavel didn't quite know what to say. So, like most, he thought it best to make small talk. But before he had to utter a word, Petro saved him.

"My dear Mrs. Nimchuk, we heard about your son's disappearance. Please know we're offering our sincerest prayers to God on his behalf."

"Thank you," she said, unable to hold back a torrent of tears. Mrs. Ponomarenko moved close and held her as her whole body quivered.

"My son. My dear sweet son. Where is he?"

A long moment passed as Pavel stood petrified. For a moment, he thought about asking, "Would you like the usual? A pound of ground beef and a breast of chicken?"

"That would be so stupid," he thought. He longed to minimize her suffering, but felt he had nothing to offer. Though he felt pity, his own soul felt empty. And so, he remained silent. Pavel's conundrum was solved when Mrs. Nimchuk, unable to compose herself, was helped out of the store. Relieved, Pavel looked at his watch. He could get out of the store soon. Since it was only thirty minutes till closing, he knew he could last that long.

"If only Savka would come home. Where is she? Where is Anna?" he wondered, tormenting himself with thoughts of their deaths. How would he find them? Maimed? Buried?

"No," he said. "I won't torment myself, at least not here. I will later, but not without a bottle."

It was now about fifteen minutes till closing. Pavel said goodbye to what he hoped would be his last customer of the day. As Pavel watched the man leave, he saw him hold the door and say, "Good afternoon, Mr. Baranov."

Vadim walked into the store. "Welcome sir," said Pavel.

"Hello."

"Is there anything in particular you're looking for?"

Vadim slowly walked by the display case, examining the various cuts of meats. "Lamb chops... I'll have lamb chops."

"Fine sir. How many will you have?"

"How about I take whatever you have left?"

"Sure."

"It looks like you're a one-man show today," said Vadim.

"Yes. I'm afraid we're a bit short-handed."

As Pavel reached down into the case, Vadim recognized him in the light, remembering his face, only he couldn't quite place it; it puzzled him.

"And how would you recommend that I prepare it?" asked Vadim.

"Well, I use a garlic and herb rub. I prepare the mix together, rub it on, then salt it lightly as it's grilled."

Then a memory came to him like a shot to the head. Vadim stared at him transfixed, and grinned.

"What is it?" asked Pavel.

"Aristotle once said, the basic human desire is to know," said Vadim.

"Yes, I have a friend who tells me that quite often," said Pavel, still wondering at the strangeness of the grin.

"Would you like to know what he said?" asked Vadim, enjoying himself as he toyed with Pavel.

"I'm sorry. Who?"

"You know! The boy! The Afghan boy!"

Pavel began to feel dizzy. Old feelings he had buried deep within him began to rise, feelings almost tactile in their quality. His face was fixed in an expression of horror. He had the look of a child lost in a department store. Without blinking, he looked into Vadim's hollow eyes, who watched him with grim fascination.

"Who are you?" whimpered Pavel slowly and gravely, barely able to get out the words.

"You know," said Vadim grinning. "We all enjoy the sausage, but not everyone enjoys how it's made."

In a flash of memory, Pavel heard the report of a submachine gun, and in vivid color, visualized the poor Afghan boy mercilessly shot in the head.

"Look what the war has done to us," said Vadim, shaking his head.

"I can only imagine what you've been carrying around with you all these years."

"You know what I've learned?" questioned Vadim.

"What's that," said Pavel.

"War doesn't determine who is right, only who is left." Then Vadim paid and walked out of the store.

Pavel was left stunned. Unable to move, barely able to breathe. His thoughts returned to the village of Charbagh: the pregnant women bayoneted to death, the heaps of burning bodies, and the young man with the red hair having the unfortunate luck to have been from that village.

In a race, Pavel turned off the lights, locked up, and walked out to his truck. As he did, it started to rain. Backing up his truck, a flash of lightning illuminated a glimpse of Stepan in his rearview mirror, causing him to hit his brakes. Pavel wanted to get home but needed his friend's wisdom. He needed to tell someone about his encounter with an old ghost.

"Hop in," said Pavel.

Just as Stepan got in, it began to pour, followed by a clap of thunder. Pavel locked his door and scanned the parking lot.

"Who are you looking for?" asked Stepan.

"The devil himself.... You wouldn't believe me if I told you."

"Try me."

Stepan listened intently as Pavel recounted, in minute detail, his encounter with Vadim. He hadn't moved his truck a bit, yet his friend was content to listen to the whole ordeal.

"Have you ever heard the legend of Siegfried?"

"No philosophy! Not right now!" yelled Pavel. "Not now!"

"It's not philosophy!" replied Stepan, apologetically.

"Really?" asked Pavel, beginning to come to his senses. Besides, he needed to get his mind off things.

"Okay. Tell me.... before I change my mind... please."

"Siegfried was a great warrior. He reforged the broken sword, 'Nothung.' Hammering away, with blackened sweat, Siegfried melded together the fragments of the broken sword upon a great anvil. He reforged 'Nothung' for the death of the fierce dragon, Fafner. The bellows blew white heat as he clanged away with his hammer until the sword was razor-sharp. Preparing for his noble quest, Siegfried tested the power of the blade. Lifting the sword high, he plunged its edge hard upon the anvil, cutting it in half."

A peal of lightning flashed as Stepan said the word 'half.'

"Then, Siegfried entered a cave where he finds Fafner guarding a horde of gold. Jumping on the dragon's back, Siegfried fought the beast, then buried the sword to the hilt in the beast's heart."

"Why are you telling me this? What does it mean?" asked Pavel.

"It means you're a broken sword my friend."

"What?"

"It's time to take the scattered fragments of your life and put them back together," said Stepan.

"What does this have to do with the story?"

"I suppose the story means something different for everyone. Considering Siegfried's quest, I suppose you could say one's metal must be proved before used. And the sword, how very much alike are we, blown by the tempest of this life's bellows, and tempered by the hammer blows of all that this world has to throw at us."

Pavel appeared unmoved by the force of his friend's attempt to enlighten him.

"Let me speak plainly. It pains me to see you like this my friend," said Stepan.

"Like what?!" snapped Pavel.

"You're afraid to really live your life!"

"I'm living my life as best as I can. What do you mean?" retorted Pavel.

"I mean your life is on permanent hold," said Stepan. "Ever since you came back from the war, you've been afraid to really live!"

Pavel found Stepan's words pregnant with meaning.

"Just remember," added Stepan, "there are tens of thousands of us Afgantsy. The war chewed us up and spit us out too!"

"I know that!" snapped Pavel.

"Look, my friend, you just have to make the best of things as they come. You have to uncomplicate yourself," said Stepan, with all the composure he could muster.

Pavel started the truck and drove Stepan to his house. Then, when he got home, he sat characteristically in his chair, and finished supper, barely saying a word to Tatyana and his wife. Afterward, he did his best to avoid everyone, wanting to be left alone with his thoughts.

Два

Wade knocked lightly on the door. It was Thursday night and he managed to find a way to leave the trench for a while. Savka appeared and let him inside. He took her in his arms and held her tightly. She closed the door and let out a deep breath, as if she had just emerged from the deep.

"I heard the shooting, and I imagined the worst," she sighed.

Staying with a friend in Zolote 3, Savka heard the firefight, which sounded like it was right outside the door. Wade had barely dropped his bag when she bombarded him with questions.

"Where can we go? When can we leave?"

He held her hands in his. "Let's take things one step at a time."

He leaned in for another kiss, but she backed away.

"I'm serious," she said.

"Me too. Life's not an exact science, it's an art."

"Every day before I met you, my governing thought was to say, life isn't hard to manage when you've nothing to lose. I've always loved that expression. All the shooting you heard, well that was just another day at the office. My goal now is to survive because I have much to lose," he said as his eyes twitched with a surge of emotion.

"How long are you going to stay here?" he asked.

"Why?"

"Well, your parents are probably scared to death!"

"You don't think I know that!" she said, backing away, plopping herself in a chair.

"I want to be with you, but we have to do this right," he said.

"What does that mean?"

"It means, I think the best thing for you and Anna right now is to be at your parents' house."

"Then what?"

Wade knelt beside her. He stared into her eyes.

"I love you. No matter what, we'll be together."

"What about Anna?"

"Her too. I love her like she was my very own! I'll find a way for us all to be together!" he promised.

"How?"

"Well, as they say, a problem well-defined and understood, is well on its way to being solved. I'll figure it out," he said, pulling her to his mouth, surprised by the fierceness of her kiss.

"I love you too! Only, don't hurt me," she said, pulling him into another intense kiss.

Savka had expectations of leaving right away. Her mind raced with crazy ideas, among which involved the three of them leaving immediately for someplace else. Anywhere but here.

"Savka, do you love me?"

"Yes!"

"Then please go home. You're safer at home. Will you go home?"

"Tomorrow," she replied, not amused with his insistence.

Wade took a Tupperware container out of his bag and put it on the table. It contained pelmeni.[1]

"Does your friend have anything to drink?" asked Wade, looking in the refrigerator, finding only a jug of milk, sandwich meat, and some condiments.

"Oh well. Shall we say grace?" summoned Wade, with a playful smile at Anna.

"You go ahead," said Savka.

---

[1] A Ukrainian fried sour cream dish.

With Anna sitting in Savka's lap, Wade said grace, "Bless us O Lord, and these Thy gifts which we are about to receive from Thy bounty, through Christ our Lord, amen."

"Where did you learn that?"

"Oh, in my travels. Isn't this what you pray?" he asked, swallowing a pelmeni whole.

"So, you were a soldier?" asked Savka.

"I was a Marine... three years. And You? Your father was a soldier?" asked Wade.

"Yes. How could you tell?"

"You just can. I don't know. I think it was the way he talked or walked... probably the way he thanked us for our service. I'm not sure."

"That reminds me, what do you have here to defend yourself?" he asked.

"Do you mean a gun?"

"Yes."

Savka left the room and returned with a rifle. "This is my grandfather's."

"An old bolt-action Mosin-Nagant," he declared with a smile.

"I haven't seen one of these in ages. It's a bolt-action antique. I bet this model sure claimed some Nazis in its hay day. I reckon that'll work."

Fueled with copious amounts of vodka, Wade finished his meal. Then it came time for him to say goodbye to Savka and Anna. "I have to work for a few days. So, I'll see you at your parents' house? Okay?"

Savka nodded, and Wade got another kiss. On his walk back to the barracks, he became aware of another presence behind him. By the occasional flashes of moonlight between clouds, Wade glanced back to see a man, no more than fifty meters on the opposite side of the road. At first, he thought nothing of it, but when he turned onto another street and still found the man behind him, he readied himself for an attack.

Wade decided to take things off-road. If the man was still there, then he would know for certain that he was being followed. Walking east, Wade crossed a footbridge, bringing him into Zolote 4. He cursed himself for having left his rifle in the barracks. But he had a blade, and it was more than suitable for most uses, including gutting hogs.

Still walking east, Wade walked on the tracks. Then the moon hid behind clouds, making it harder for Wade to see the man. Looking for better defensive ground, Wade crossed to the other side of the road, and walked between two apartments that were well lit. Wade could feel the man at his heels. He stopped and whirled around, facing off with the man who was now a scant ten meters away.

"Nice night for a stroll?" commented Wade.

The man, who appeared to be twenty-something, wore a brown leather jacket, and gave no reply. He had stopped momentarily, but then began to close the gap on Wade. Unflinchingly, he pulled out a knife, its long-curved blade gleamed in the moonlight.

"It's like that huh?" shrugged Wade.

The man's knife flashed as he took up an icepick grip. He lunged at Wade, intending to plunge the knife's edge into Wade's carotid arch. Wade raised his left arm, blunting the man's thrust.

In a fury, Wade delivered two rapid right punches to the man's temple. Stunned, the man bent forward, and Wade brought down a vicious piledriver elbow thrust to the back of the man's head, causing him to drop the blade, crunching him to the ground.

Right where he wanted him, Wade turned to run off. Undeterred, the man staggered to his feet, wiped the blood from his nose, then cleared a pistol from under his jacket. He took careful aim at Wade's face.

"BOOM!"

Wade grunted and shook. Wiping the man's blood off his face, Wade watched the man slowly fall face down onto the ground, revealing Savka standing a few feet behind him, the rifle in her hands belching out a whiff of smoke from the barrel.

"Oh my God! Wade, are you okay?" shrieked Savka frantically, as her hands began to shake, nearly dropping the rifle.

"I saw him follow you, and it looked like he would give you trouble. I guess I was right!"

"Well, you sure filled that guy's head with lead."

"Who was he?" asked Savka.

"Who knows? Let's get you back to the house. I'll go back to work in the morning," he said as the two of them ran down the street.

Три

It was late Thursday night; Alonso, Danylo, and Oleksandr were out in the strongpoint, which was basically a hole in the ground covered with camouflage netting. A Coleman lantern swayed in the breeze, illuminating the floor of the bunker; a cozy ten by ten enclosure. On the floor, a series of rotting boards kept the soldiers a few inches away from the mud. On one of the log walls holding back the earth, a single poster hung next to a battery-operated wall clock with hour and minute hands. Danylo stood up, holding a pair of binoculars outfitted with two telescopic lenses. These enabled him to observe the field out to their front.

"What can you see?" asked Ivan.

"Not much," said Danylo.

"Well how would you, without night vision goggles!" said Ivan to Alonso.

"The U.S. gave us thermal night vision goggles and javelins, just so they could collect dust in a warehouse somewhere in Kharkiv!"

"Really? Is that true Ivan?" asked Alonso, sitting on the ammo crate he'd claimed as his own.

"Yes, it is!" said Ivan, throwing up his hand in a comedic way.

"Don't worry Ivan, that cat will show up before there's any shooting," said Danylo, laughing maniacally.

"Not the cat joke again!"

"How will we know if the rebels are in the field?" asked Alonso, with an expression as serious as a heart attack.

"We have some barbed wire about a hundred meters out that has some cans tied to it," said Ivan.

"And a cat," added Oleksandr.

"Will you shut up about that cat!"

"How long is this shift?" asked Alonso.

"Till six o'clock," said Ivan.

"Oh my God, this is going to be a long one!" said Oleksandr, lifting his butt off his stool to cut a loud fart.

"Can't you fart out there?" asked Ivan pointing to the trench.

"I can't help it. We've had beans three nights in a row!" Ivan's cellphone buzzed.

"It's Wade. He's saying he'll be back in the morning," said Ivan, typing a reply.

"What are you telling him?" asked Danylo.

"What else would I say? I said, 'we got things under control.'"

"What a dog! He's with that blue-haired vixen," said Danylo.

"She'll give him a run for his money," said Oleksandr.

"No. She's no whore," said Ivan. "Your mind only works one way! Wade said she's his María, but not his Catherine."

"I don't understand," said Oleksandr.

"Neither do I. But make no mistake, I've been with Wade since the Battle of Ilovaisk in 2014. He's a good man who would never take advantage of a lady. I tell you, he's stir-crazy for her. He'll end up settling down with this one. Just you wait and see," said Ivan.

Четыре

It was the wee hours of Friday morning. The moon's waning gibbous cast a shadow of a solitary figure walking along the bank of the Komyshuvakha River. Overlooking the bank, in a clearing amongst a clump of trees, a small pyre burned, casting long shadows. The river flowed on, gurgling like an old man. Just over the sound of the river could be heard the gentle snorting of a horse, playfully galloping in a nearby field. Vadim waded shirtless into the cool water, his back covered in scars. He ritualistically washed his hands, then held up a long knife. Its curved edge gleamed in the pale moonlight. As the last residue of blood flowed free from his blade and onto his hand into the river, he looked up at the vast sea of stars, and prayed.

"On this sacred day, O Perun, god of thunder, lightning, rain, and of war, the one striking the oak, making it sacred, receive this sacrifice from mine hands. May you be satiated with this blood. Long ago, the Hebrew God drove you out of these lands. May this river run red with blood and these cities burst into flames, until your worship is restored."

As he waded out of the river and onto the shore, off in the distance could be heard the faint howl of a wolf, followed by a crackling of gunfire. Both sounds blended and echoed in the surrounding hills.

12

The Discovery

"**Good** and evil; you never have one without the other," thought Pavel. "And it's always where you never expect it."

It was Friday morning. As Pavel got ready for work, all he could do is think about Savka and Anna, and his mysterious visitor in the butcher shop.

"Perhaps he was only a figment of my tormenting anxiety," thought Pavel. "Maybe he was a ghost from my past, or perhaps he was sent to torment me for my past sins."

Sitting at the dining room table, he took his breakfast with his father: black tea and a bowl of porridge kasha. It was now the second day since his daughters had disappeared. Tormenting himself, he imagined the very worst had befallen them. "Where are they? Killed by a stray bullet, I just know it!" he thought as he made small talk with his father.

"She's here in town," said Yelizaveta.

"You hope. You always hope for the best. The world is dark, evil, and unforgiving, and people are completely ignorant. You think people are basically good. I say they are basically bad."

Vasyli continued to eat, quietly contenting himself to stay out of the discussion.

"I'd do anything for our little Anna; the world will chew her up and spit her out as refuse. I know the world! I've seen men at their very worst!" exclaimed Pavel, with a light thump on the table.

"That's why I expect the worst," he muttered, scooping the last spoonful of porridge. His wife sat quietly as he harangued her. His conscience struck him, and he felt sorry as soon as he said it. "I'm sorry love," he said, hugging her.

"It will be alright; I just know it. Have faith," she said.

"Okay," he replied, as Tatyana walked back into the kitchen. Like most mornings, she had gotten up earlier to leave. Working at a bakery necessitated such early starts. After having her breakfast, which consisted of a slice of black bread and butter with a cup of tea, she rushed out the door with her bags in hand, while texting a friend. It would be a short, five-minute walk to the bakery. Walking and glancing down at her phone, she enjoyed the cool morning air. She listened to the sound of her shoes on the pavement, watching the trees sway with the breeze. Then, she froze and let out a blood-curdling scream.

"Oh my God!" cried Yelizaveta, recognizing the voice of Tatyana.

Pavel threw on his shoes. His mind raced with a dozen terrible thoughts as he flew down the stairs, nearly killing himself as he missed the last few steps. Reaching the bottom floor, he was shocked to find Tatyana in a three-way hug with Savka and little Anna. His eyes were huge with amazement. Waves of anxiety, anger, and terror all flashed over him in a torrent of emotions. Then, he did what any distraught father would do – he ran and embraced them all.

"My daughters! My dear daughters! Thanks be to God!"

Pavel reached out for Anna and took her in his arms, kissing her cheeks. Pressing her little body to his chest, he gave her a big hug as she let out a little squeal.

"My sweet little Anna, I thought I lost you forever!" Savka stood by, unsure of what to do.

"Come here, my dear," said Pavel, drawing her to himself, embracing her tightly. "I thought I lost you!"

The clamor of shoes down the steps brought Yelizaveta and Vasyli. "My darlings!" exclaimed Yelizaveta.

"Father," said Pavel, pulling him into the group hug. There, they stood in a long embrace.

"I imagined, the very worst, but here you are," said Pavel, enraptured with a sense of home as he waved consolingly to some onlookers, who were peering down the hallway.

"Tatyana, I heard screaming. What happened?" Yelizaveta asked in a sour tone.

"I saw Victor hanging in a tree," she said, in shocked disbelief.

"What? Where?" asked Vasyli.

"He's just down the road, there," she said, pointing to a tree about a hundred meters away.

"Okay. Everyone go up to the apartment. Father and I will go. Okay?" ushered Pavel.

Pavel and Vasyli cleared the steps and ran down the road to find Victor, hanging from a tree within sight of their apartment.

"He was hanged as we slept," said Vasyli.

His lifeless body dangled a mere six inches off the ground. Vasyli gritted his teeth and cursed. Then, he pulled off his shirt and wrapped it around Victor's mangled body. He held him while Pavel took out a knife and cut the rope, dropping him to the ground. Vasyli bent down to check his pulse, half hoping he was still alive. Victor's hands were bound behind his back; his naked body bore signs of torture. Despite the grisliness, what caught Pavel's eye the most was the conspicuous mark of a stab wound in Victor's chest.

"No doubt the death blow," thought Pavel.

"Who would do such a thing?" asked Vasyli, holding up Victor's left hand to discover four missing fingernails.

"You would have made a fine husband for my granddaughter," said Vasyli under his breath.

"Tatyana loved him. I loved him," said Vasyli, as he began to weep bitterly.

Feeling both horror at the sight of Victor and elation over the return of Savka and Anna, Pavel stood there in silence, not knowing what to say. "I had high hopes for him too," said Pavel with a furrowed brow.

"Should I get the police?" asked Pavel, only half sure of what to do. Vasyli held Victor's head gently, staring into the emptiness of his face.

"I'll go," said Pavel. His mind racing with thoughts.

"Two days ago," thought Pavel, "I was on the edge of eternity; today, I have my life back!"

"Father," said Pavel, several times until he got his attention, "I don't know what the future holds; all I know is that I want us to have a future. I'll go in for us today. You can stay home. Okay?"

"Okay, son," Vasyli said, smiling proudly through a sob.

Два

Pavel had a newfound sense of purpose. Within an hour, he reported what happened to Victor and arrived at the butchery in record time. Driving up, he found several customers waiting outside. He apologized for being late, let them in, and quickly readied the shop. He tried to process all that he was feeling: Two terrible nights virtually without sleep, the return of his daughters, and Victor's brutal murder. What surprised him the most was that he no longer felt a gnawing sense to leave. Instead, what he found in its place was a growing sense of righteous indignation.

"Why would anyone murder Victor?"

"How old such a question has become...?" he thought.

"My father is right," he said to himself. "It's time to stand up or there won't be anything left to fight for." The clarity and forcefulness of his thoughts surprised him. Morning passed as Pavel managed the store alone. Customers came and went. Soon, it was afternoon, and Father Malashenko arrived.

"I heard what happened to Victor," said the priest.

It was customary for priests to make their rounds to assuage others, only, Pavel wasn't in the mood.

"Yet another young man murdered in this stupid little town. May the Lord have mercy on the man who did that. For I won't. What do you say to that, Father? Are murderers entitled to mercy?"

"There's a world of difference between killing and murder," said the priest.

"I realize that," replied Pavel curtly.

"How many more young men must die in this Godforsaken town, before people get off the fence?" remarked Pavel.

"My father is right! The only thing necessary for the triumph of evil, is for good men to do nothing. Up till now, I've done nothing! Everything ends in blood and fire. All men are basically evil!"

"The world is not all bad," said the priest.

"Have you seen the body, Father?"

"My friend, as they say, whoever fights monsters should see to it that in the process, he doesn't become a monster."

"No sermons now, priest," said Pavel sharply before returning to his work. For a long moment, Pavel did his best to ignore Father Malashenko, who stood silently on the other side of the counter. Pavel's conscience struck him.

"Forgive me, Father."

"What's to forgive, my son? Pavel, I mean you no disrespect. I just want to help."

"I know. You're a good priest. You're God's gift to us."

"For me, it's an honor to serve. Well... I must go to Victor's house," said the priest, glancing down at his watch, "His mother needs me."
Pavel then bowed his head as Father Malashenko raised his hands in a benediction.

"Just between you and I," said the priest, "I'd love to have a wedding instead of another funeral."

"Thank you for coming by, Father," said Pavel. He was alone again. Pavel's thoughts then returned to his daughters, and his family's safety. Closing up took less than ten minutes; Pavel packed the meats away in the freezer, wiped the counters, locked up the store, and drove home.

All day long, he had contemplated the simple life of living and growing old with his family around him. He felt foolish for dismissing such a gift. As he entered the apartment foyer, the delicious aromas of his wife's cooking carried him upstairs. "What a change one day can bring," he thought while, sprinting up the stairs.

Pavel found his home just as it was before the disaster. It was exactly what he longed for. His whole family together at the table, enjoying his wife's good food. Soon, the meal was over, and the family retired to the living room. Pavel kissed his wife, and then sat down in his chair, sipping his black tea. "Stepan," he thought, "you're right. Man conquers the world by conquering himself. I must make the best of things in my power, and influence what's not." That night, Pavel decided he would stay.

Три

It was Friday evening, and Alonso was free for his first weekend pass. He could now put his monotonous trench life on hold until Sunday morning. He borrowed a car and drove to the Wolf's Lair. On the way there, all he could think about was Zlata. Pulling up, he saw the neon sign and heard the muffled noise of carousing above the pulsating music of the discotheque. Like all clubs of the sort, the Wolf's Lair offered a coalescence of music, drinks, and scantily clad young ladies. All of which served like a drug to languorously overdose the synapses of a soldier's brain. Stepping out of the car, Alonso saw three men, obviously drunk, stumble out of a car and head for the club. Entering the club, he was met with the overpowering aroma of beer, perfume, hairspray, and cigarette smoke.

Walking further inside, he discovered a mixture of night people: Soldiers at varying levels of intoxication, disintegrating couples, and a few hookers. Walking past a dancing couple and several soldiers, he sat down at the bar next to Zlata and uncoiled himself. He took in the sight of her, a tight top and miniskirt. He pulled her close to him, tasting her lipstick. The music was loud, but they could still hear each other talk.

"Where have you been?" asked Zlata. "It's been days."

"Ah you missed me! I wasn't sure."

The bartender came by and stood before Alonso. "Give him a drink... something strong," she said.

"Vodka?" predicted the bartender.

"Sure."

"Look," said Zlata, "I think something big is about to happen."

"What do you mean?" he asked, as he pressed her close to his chest. He leaned in to kiss her again, but she pulled away. "I need to tell you this."

"Okay, tell me."

"Last week, one of Dimitri's goons was here. A tall Russian. A real creep. He was here overnight. Anyway, while he was on the toilet, I overheard him talking to Dimitri."

"Who is Dimitri?"

"He owns this dump."

"Anyway, I didn't make out exactly what was said, but he kept using the name Wagner, and something about rockets."

Alonso lit a cigarette and sat pensively on the barstool. He took a deep drag. "Wagner you say?"

"Does that name mean anything to you?" she asked.

"Maybe, if he meant Wagner Group. I've read about them, they're mercs. They're Putin's private army. They've been busy in Crimea and Syria, and I guess they're here now. Huh, why wouldn't they be?" he said, not remotely fazed.

"Okay gorgeous, you told me. Now come here," he said, pulling on her arm.

"Wait. There's more," she balked, pulling herself free.

"Come on, give me a break!" he said, picking up his drink and finishing it in a gulp.

"There's another guy that Dimitri talks to a lot. His name is Vadim. I saw him in here once. He gave me the creeps. I swear, he's the devil's son-in-law."

"Baby, why are you telling me this?"

"Because they control everything in this town. You name it!"

A burly soldier sat down next to Zlata and put his hand on her thigh. "Hey, baby."

Without taking her eyes off Alonso, she slapped his hand away. "Piss off!"

Unrelentingly, the burly man grabbed her elbow.

"She said piss off!" blurted Alonso, standing up, towering over the other man.

"Look," continued Zlata, "you don't know these guys. They're tied in with the mafia. Their greatest hits include black marketing, car bombing, assassinations, you name it! Do you see these women?" she asked, motioning with her hand around the bar. "They're all strung out on opium. That's Dimitri's specialty. Nothing happens here without their say so. They even know where you sleep. Doesn't that bother you?"

"Baby, stop worrying," said Alonso, unphased. "Can't we talk about this upstairs?"

Not getting through to him, she turned away, tucking her hair behind her ears.

"Okay. So, you're right. They control everything. This place is corrupt. What else is new?" he asked, sliding her barstool around so she faced him again.

"What do you want me to do about it?" asked Alonso, softly tracing his hand over her shoulder.

"You're a soldier. You're supposed to help. You're here to protect us."

"I shoot people I never see on the other side of a field. You want me to kill your boss and these other goons?"

"Why not?" she said, "They're killing you. You just haven't realized it yet!"

"How about going to the police?"

"Sure. They can perform the autopsies after we're all dead."

"Okay, I'll tell my boss. Will that make you happy?"

"Yes, I suppose."

"But not until Sunday morning. Tonight, let's have a good time," he said, motioning for her to go upstairs. Alonso's persistence prevailed. She grabbed his hand and led him away from the bar, guiding him up a flight of narrow stairs to her room. Nothing about it was remarkable. The walls were bare, except for a long thin mirror, and a window opposite the door. Alonso felt sorry for not listening as he should. "We can talk about it more if you'd like."

"Shut up," she said, as she turned off the lights. Then she kissed him passionately. After a long moment they broke, neglecting to breathe. Then she dove in for another kiss, like a mermaid plunging into the deepest sea.

Later that night, Alonso told her about his life in Sevilla. He was curious to learn that she didn't know about the bullfights. They talked late into the night and into early morning.

"Look," she said, "last year, my friend Nadia was approached by this guy, I don't know his name. She was really pretty, so, the guy promised her easy money and a career in showbusiness... and she bought it."

"I never saw her again.... For all I know, she's in Istanbul 'working' in a place like this. I don't want to end up like her. I don't want to keep living like this."

"Would you take me away from here? Would you take me to your Spain?" She glanced over to see that Alonso was already asleep. She touched his face tenderly, as if they were longtime lovers, and pulled the sheet over him.

13

Fifth Column

Men don't learn from history. This is perhaps the most important lesson that history has to teach. History shows us what to avoid by pointing out the most common mistakes that mankind is apt to make and to repeat. The wise learn from the experience of fools, yet fools learn only from their own mistakes. Men, such as the separatists, don't want to die any more than other men defending their beliefs; yet only time would tell if they were anything more than a mere fifth column for Moscow to contemplate its next move.

It was Friday night. While the last of the miners at Kobalt Two had gone home for the weekend, Vadim and Dimitri were inside the director's office sharing drinks.

Sitting at the table, Vadim opened a bottle of vodka and poured two glasses.

"The fireworks will begin soon," said Vadim, raising his glass in a toast.

"You're in a rather capital mood."

"Shouldn't I be? I came here to monopolize the coal-mining industry and I did. This town has been a real gold mine... Za zda-ró-vye!"[1]

"Za zda-ró-vye!" echoed Dimitri, as he clinked his glass with Vadim's.

"And things are about to become even more lucrative," pledged Vadim.

"How so?"

"Fire consumes fuel, but liberates smoke."

Unable to quite grasp the meaning, Dimitri looked at him curiously.

"This operation will most certainly fail."

"Really?" asked Dimitri.

"Yes, but that's ok.

"It is?"

"It's okay, because this is how we play the game."

"What about bringing the town into the LPR?" asked Dimitri, now puzzled.

"My friend, you've been using too much of your own product! Zolote under the LPR again? Why, that would lose business for us."

"I don't quite get your meaning," said Dimitri.

---

[1] To your health!

"My friend, chaos is good for business! Do you understand? Chaos is our business. We create the problem, then we sell the cure."

"What of Oleg and the Druzhina?" asked Dimitri.

"Fuel for the fire!" dismissed Vadim, shaking his head as he raised his glass for another toast, "Fuel for the fire!"

"Another Oleg will take his place, who will raise another Druzhina, and so on, and so on, and so on..."

"I see," said Dimitri.

"Now, my friend," said Vadim, taking a long draught of vodka, "I've got work to do in Sudan."

"Za zda-ró-vye!" he said, clinking his glass with Dimitri's.

"I want you to manage things."

"I see. You want me to be Mr. Black?"

"Naturally. Do you think you can manage?"

"I think so."

"Once a week, you'll report to M____. Do you think you can handle that?"

"Okay," said Dimitri, pensively holding his glass.

"Now, there is a lot involved in the fine art of creating chaos. Let me offer you a bit of advice. First and foremost, always kill your way out of a problem. When in doubt, liquidate. Dispense of a problem as it arises."

"That's simple enough," said Dimitri.

"Second, don't lose sight of the overall goal. Our bloodletting is for the people to equate death and pain with the Ukrainian government's presence. Make them feel like they're getting shot at a wedding, because people are fighting over the music... chaos is your friend. We must maintain a careful balance. And the kopankas are the key to keeping the people. With the mayor and the police chief out of the picture, I'd say the only one prying into our business is the OSCE. A close second is the Army, but they're oblivious to our designs, contented to remain on the mere periphery."

Vadim continued to wax eloquently, "Third, continue to massage our contact in the OSCE. You've done well so far! Money and the creature comforts of your little house of ill repute should handle things. As you know, men are easy to manipulate," he said taking a cigar and lighting it.

"And so, whatever you do, don't lose that poof house."
Dimitri's belly giggled like jelly as he laughed.

"Fourth, perhaps this is not in any real order... but importantly, hide in plain sight. It's so easy in this line of work to become a recluse; don't."

"Finally, as they say in the army, 'victory has many fathers, but defeat is an orphan.' In clandestine work, if you succeed, no one is aware. If you fail, your house of cards comes down on you. No one comes to your aid, yet disavows your very existence... za zda-ró-vye!"

"Za zda-ró-vye!" returned Dimitri.

"Before you go, there's one thing I'd like to know," said Dimitri.

"What's that?"

"How did you ever get out of that Afghan cave?"

"Hmm. Gorgan told you about it, did he?" questioned Vadim. "It was the Spring of 1987. The war in

Afghanistan was winding down, and the generals were looking for an exit strategy; that is, one that didn't involve outright humiliation."

"I was also there in Kandahar, in 1987," said Dimitri.

"Hmm. We launched our operations out of there," said Vadim pensively.

"As you know, the CIA's funding of the mujahideen, and their bringing in of Stinger missiles, was taking quite a toll on us. Armed with the Stingers, the Afghan fighters brought down over two dozen Mi-24 Hinds in the first year alone. Well, that's how my last raid got botched."

"Was that when it was?"

"Yes. It was the last week of May. We flew out of Kandahar with some of our Afghan army counterparts. It was supposed to be a sweep of a lightly fortified area... we flew east on the edge of the red desert toward Spin Buldak and into a hornet's nest. The Mi-8 helicopter I was on got shot out of the sky. Somehow, I survived the impact. I awoke to the sharp smell of piss, finding myself in a cave. Have you ever smelled a mujahideen cave?"

"Yes. Like goats in a sewer," said Dimitri.

"Very much indeed. Well, I was there something like three days, in and out of consciousness, murmuring the words 'under the stars of Jalalabad, we cursed our damned war.'"

"My hands were bound behind me; you know, like this," said Vadim, indicating a position in which one's hands are tied behind their back while suspended by a rope.

"They call it strappado, I think. There was another man captured along with me, a pilot. He begged for his life. They clubbed him to death on the first day. But me, I spit on the floor of the cave and cursed their mothers."

"Each day the beatings grew worse, along with the smell. Every morning a bearded man in a black turban, whose name I've forgotten, beat me for an hour as I hanged from a pole in that dreaded position. Finally, they dropped me to the floor of the cave as I writhed in pain. He didn't want to know anything, he just wanted to break my will. Hah!"

"Well, late on the third day, another Red Army column passed through the hills near the cave I was in. The army column made such a ruckus that the idiots holding me captive went to the mouth of the cave to watch the fireworks... Well, I managed to get free from my bonds and found a rifle, then they were history! But they did manage to give me something to remember them by," he said pointing to the savage scar on his right cheek.

"The bearded man in the black turban gave me this as a souvenir."

"What did you do to him?" asked Dimitri.

"With him, I took my time."

"Now, my friend, I leave you with the money, all two hundred thousand of it that we recovered the other day."

Vadim raised his glass.

"Za zda-ró-vye! Until we meet again on the lush green pastures of Nav."

Then, clinking his glass with Dimitri's, he said, "Mischief, thou art afoot. Take what course thou wilt."

Два

The soldier heard a car approach and he sat up. His legs cracked as he stretched them out. The floor he had slept on the night before was hard. From what he could tell, he was being held in a room of an abandoned mine. He would have tried to leave, had it not been for the zip ties binding his hands and feet. Besides that, the day before he could hear someone outside the door, no doubt guarding him. He had eaten a little the day before, but by now his stomach growled with hunger. He heard footsteps coming up the stairs outside; the door opened. It was Father Mitka in his black clerical cossack, identifying himself as a married priest.

"Soldier."

"Yes, Father."

"I hope what I brought you was sufficient."

"Yes, Father. Thank you for the food and water."

"What are you going to do with me?" asked the soldier.

"I don't know," said the priest, motioning with his hand for them to talk quietly. "Where are you from, my son?"

"Dnipro."

"What is your faith?"

"Same as yours. Orthodox."

"I've been to Dnipro. What a beautiful city. I once visited Taras Shevchenko Park. Have you been there?" asked the priest.

"No, but I plan on doing a lot of things if I get out of here. Am I getting out of here?" asked the soldier.

"What did they do to you?" asked the priest.

"A man asked me a lot of questions."

"About what exactly?"

"Are you with them?" asked the soldier, while stretching his legs.

"A man asked me about our shifts in the trench... Forgive me Father, but why are you here?"

"I'm here because I cannot stand idly by any longer."

"I don't understand," said the soldier, as the priest took out a knife.

"Don't worry, my son," he said as he cut him free.

"Freeing you, frees my conscience. Now, come with me, my son."

"What about the guard?"

"He's gone. Let's get you home."

As Father Mitka walked down into the parking lot, he sensed a release from his guilt. As he reached his car, he opened the trunk. "You'd better ride in here until we're out of town," he said.

"Okay, Father," said the soldier reluctantly, as he climbed into the trunk.

Father Mitka closed the trunk, then looking up to heaven, he said, "Forgive me, Lord."

As he did, the frightful baying of his conscience was finally appeased. However, Father Mitka failed to see Gorgan sitting in a car on the other side of the lot. The priest got in his car and turned the ignition. As he did, he set off the explosive device Gorgan had placed under the hood. A flash of fire was followed by a deafening explosion, as the car went up in a ball of flames. Staggering out of the seething inferno onto his knees, Father Mitka howled with impotent rage. His eyes looked over at Gorgan, standing motionless, watching him burn like a human candle. Then, Gorgan drove off.

Три

Colonel Kerlikowski's men assembled at the mouth of the mine, known as Kobalt 4. Off to the west, they could hear Father Mitka's car exploded. Keenly aware of noise and light, being in such proximity to the line of contact, the thirty-five men of Kerlikowski's so-called 'Phantom Battalion' stealthily approached the mine's entrance. Breaking the threshold, they were met with the pungent odor of methane.

Flashlight in hand, Kerlikowski led the way into the cavernous abyss of the mineshaft. The light barely pierced the darkness. As he went, his flashlight revealed the mysteries of the subterranean world. Every few meters, he encountered support beams holding up the roof. The floor of the shaft was obstacle-laden, mixed with standing water. Along the way, deeper into the mine, bits of broken machinery littered the floor, along with garbage, and leaves. Their boots shuffled along the rock surface and kicked the loose items, which echoed throughout the shaft.

The further they went into the mine, the lower the ceiling became. At one point, the men had to crouch, or duck-walk, as the roof lowered to just over a meter in height. Encumbered by their ammo-laden packs, kit, and guns, the going was slow. All told, it took nearly two hours to navigate the four hundred meters. At the midpoint, Kerlikowski encountered the next obstacle, noxious fumes combined with the scent of rotting flesh.

"My God, what is that stench?" he asked.

Men gagged at the overpowering pungency. In the lead, Kerlikowski made out the shapes of heaps along the floor. The heaps were bodies. Lying face down with their hands bound, the bodies of six men bore signs of execution. They appeared to have been dead for several days. Kerlikowski placed his sleeve over his mouth and nose and continued to press on.

"Keep moving," he said, nearly gagging as he spoke the words. He wanted to get out for the stench, but somehow they would have to bear it, at least until dawn. They had infiltrated into the government-held zone, passing under the trench line. Illuminated by the eerie red glow of flashlights, dressed in sterile combat fatigues with no identity insignias, the men of the Phantom Battalion made their final checks, poised for what they believed would be the defining moment of their lives.

Четыре

Pavel had just finished another fine dinner. "Every meal at this house is a feast," he thought. Adjourning to the living room to have his tea, his thoughts turned to Father Malashenko. The coarse words he had uttered to the priest rang in his ears. He needed to clear his conscience and wondered if it was too late to visit. The priest didn't have a phone; he didn't believe in them. After a short discussion with his wife and daughters regarding the living habits of orthodox priests, Pavel decided on a Friday night visit. "It isn't too late. He'll see me," Pavel said to himself, walking down to his truck.

He took the road north and then west, instead of the more direct route to avoid silhouetting himself on his drive at night. The separatists were known to fire at cars at night near the gray zone. It took only ten minutes for Pavel to arrive in the courtyard of the old church. Pavel knocked softly on the door of the hermitage. Father Malashenko came to the door. "I apologize for this late visit," said Pavel. "I disrespected you. Please forgive me Father."

"My son, you came here just to tell me that? There's nothing to forgive. Please come in. Have some tea. I just boiled some water."

Pavel followed the priest to his study and took a seat. He enjoyed the familiarity of it all, feeling at home in the priest's study. Father Malashenko handed him a cup of tea, "Here is some sugar and cream, if you like... no, you like it black, isn't that so?"

"Yes. Ever since my army days," replied Pavel.

"Me too," noted the priest.

"You were in the Red Army?" questioned Pavel with a look of surprise.

"Yes. Like you, I once served the Kremlin."

"In Afghanistan?" asked Pavel, curiously amazed.

"Yes. Before the Lord called me to be a priest, I was an intelligence officer in the Red Army. I spent two years in Kabul. But unlike you, I'm happy to say, I never left the base."

Not knowing what to say, Pavel sipped his tea, utterly amazed at the revelation. An uncomfortable silence followed. Pavel looked up at the icon of St. George and the dragon, then back at the priest. He just couldn't believe it. Then he thought, "You sent us to our deaths!"

Father Malashenko broke the silence. "That was long ago, and I was a different man then. That man is dead. Every now and then I see him, but he is dead nonetheless."

Pavel could think of nothing else to say, so he said "amen." Glancing at Pavel's arm, Father Malashenko noted the strange bruising. He didn't want to pry into Pavel's personal life, but he felt he had to ask. Pavel realized his concern. Before he had a chance, Pavel said, "This happens sometimes. It began my second year in Afghanistan," he said, pulling back on his sleeve, revealing a long series of black and purple patches of swollen skin.

"Really? How exactly?" queried Father Malashenko.

"Well, it was the last month that I was in that Godforsaken country. It was in the summer. It was hot and our commander had just ordered us to push our defenses further out to gain more breathing room," he said, pausing, thinking whether or not he should continue.

"Please go on," urged the priest.

"As we kept digging, you know, you find so much when you dig. Well, we came across some things that was better left uncovered."

"What was it?"

"A burial. A mass burial. Judging from the state of the bodies, I'd say they were executed, then laid in rows."

"How many?"

"Something like two thousand."

"My God," said the priest, as he watched Pavel's arm hair stand straight up.

"Are you okay, my son?"

Pavel nodded.

"I'm sorry. I don't mean to pry."

"Apparently, we unearthed a great massacre that we promptly covered again, then went about our business. Living there after uncovering it made the place something of a conduit of the supernatural."

Pavel raised his arm, "This began that day."

"At night, strange things could be heard. Things got so bad that over the following several weeks, we had four men in my company kill themselves. They couldn't stand to hear the voices any longer. I came home later that year, and all seemed well, till the night came, and the dreams came."

In an instant, the atmosphere around Pavel turned ominously dark, as if he sat on the very edge of the eternal shadowy realm. A candle in the study flickered, then was snuffed out. Pavel sensed a familiar tightness of chest. He shuddered. Sweat began to pour from his head. His heart palpitated and he grew dizzy. Overcome with dread, he dropped his cup. The remaining tea splattered onto the floor, and the sound of the cup breaking echoed through the open door and down the hall.

"It's okay Pavel. The war is over."

Pavel sat forward and put his hands over his face. "It will never be over. It will never be over," he said in languished panic.

As Pavel travailed with angst, the room grew otherworldly with a fearsome darkness. The priest sensed an evil presence. The corner of the room behind Pavel became pitch-black, as if a black hole had opened. Within the shadowy recesses, by the light of the remaining candle, the priest saw a cloaked shape standing behind Pavel. Its presence brought with it a malodorous scent, like that of something old that had been carelessly unearthed. Its eyes burned with an unholy light, and its appearance was like that of a floating cloak of darkness that spread its wings around the room.

"Be gone," said the priest as he stood up, holding out the cross that he carried around his neck.

"No. I have authority over him," shrilled the demon in a voice that made the hairs on the priest's arm stand up.

"What's your name?" asked Father Malashenko.

"I am Svabog," proclaimed the demon with devious satisfaction. "I once sired giants. I taught you men all manner of murderous arts and spells. I have wandered the earth for six millennia and have waylaid thousands in my wake, and this is my current host. I've followed him from the Hindu Kush.... I have authority over him."

"Not anymore," declared the priest.

"Hah!" refuted the demon, laughing with hellish pleasure.

Then the priest began to pray, "Kuriye Iesu Christeh Elehson meh."[2]

The demon growled and hissed, baring its teeth.

The priest continued to intone the words, "Kuriye Iesu Christeh Elehson meh. Kuriye Iesu Christeh Elehson meh."

The demon became frantic, "Stop praying!" he hissed, cursing bitterly.

"This is The Jesus Prayer; it burns demons!" exclaimed the priest. Grabbing a bottle of holy water, he opened it, and doused the corner of the room, causing the demon to writhe and curse in terror. The demon threw a vase, shattering it on the wall.

"Stop praying!" shrieked the malignant spirit, tossing over a side table.

"I'll kill him!" The demon let out a low guttural growl.

"Kuriye Iesu Christeh Elehson meh.... leave him and never come back! I consign you to the abyss. You have no authority over him, by the power of Christ!" exclaimed the priest.

Father Malashenko continued to pray for another few minutes until he could sense the black cloud that hovered over Pavel, leached away. The room fell silent,

---

[2] Lord Jesus Christ, have mercy on me.

and a settled peace fell on Pavel. Then the priest watched over him, as he sat back in the chair and slept.

After about an hour, Pavel awoke to find Father Malashenko reading his Bible.

"Are you okay, my son?"

"Yes!" said Pavel, sensing a great clarity of mind. His desperation vanished, becoming as distant as a faded memory. The future seemed wide-open and unbound.

"Was I demon possessed?"

"No. Oppressed. Believers cannot be demon possessed, though they may be oppressed and afflicted."

"You had apparently opened a door for this demon to oppress you. I have shut it, but you must keep that door closed."

"What door is that?"

"It varies by person and problem. For some, the door is alcohol or some other kind of addiction. For others, it's anxiety or depression, or pornography."

"What was it for me?"

"I'm not entirely sure. But what I want you to remember is that the Church is under God's theocracy. Christ is our King, and whenever you are in trouble, pray The Jesus Prayer. 'Kuriye Iesu Christeh Elehson meh.' Try praying it."

"Okay," said Pavel, taking the words of the ancient prayer on his lips. With a look on his face like one of the magi perceiving the infant Deliverer, Pavel sensed himself gaining strength with each iteration.

"Yes. Good," affirmed the priest.

Pavel wiped the tears from his face, and intimating that he would leave, he said, "I don't know how I can ever thank you, Father."

"Serving Christ's flock is my reward, my son."

Then, with a prescience that stunned Pavel, he said, "I don't know what you have in mind to do, but I want you to remember, a true warrior fights not because he hates what is in front of him, but because he loves what is behind him."

"I'll remember that, Father. Thank you."

"I have one for you, Father."

"Yes, what is it my son?"

"We cannot do evil that good may come..."

"True."

"But we may have to do violence in the cause of good."

Father Malashenko smiled deeply. "Well said, my friend. Well said."

14

Threshold of Violence

To desire mere riches has never been the lure of war, rather to be richer than others. It's the humdrum, age-old paradox of the haves and have nots.

It was a clear blue Saturday morning, not a cloud in sight. Wade, Ivan, and Bogdan were out in the trench line. It was about six o'clock. Wade was just finishing his first cup of coffee. Taking in a rush of air, he stretched and yawned the sleep from his body, touching off the involuntary reflex that hit the others around him in a spasmic wave. Unbeknownst to them, Kerlikowski and Marko's men were only a few hundred meters away. The Phantom Battalion had spent all night hiding and sweating in the mine. Just before dawn, they linked up with Marko's men, then moved to a position just north of strongpoint 3.

Wade and the others listened to Bogdan wax philosophically about European politics. He would tend to ramble on. So much so that, most of the time, Wade would feign to have something else to do and wander off, saving himself from the endless prattle. Just then, the wind shifted so that it came from the north. Wade detected the pungency of body odor and sweat-laden uniforms. By now, Marko and Kerlikowski's ripe troops had closed to a mere two-hundred meters away from the strongpoint and were poised to strike.

"Hey, hey, hey" said Wade, in a dull whisper. Crouching down, his body language cued them in to the imminent threat behind them. "Spread out."

Seconds later, dozens of guns crackled and burst – THWACK! THWACK! THWACK! A sandbag next to Wade's face exploded in a shower of earth. Round after round struck the strongpoint, ripping through the sandbags, and splintering the tops the planks. KABOOOM! An RPG-7 warhead exploded, knocking Wade to the floor of the trench and showering him with dirt.

Ivan grabbed the stock of his PKM, white-knuckled and spinning around, he repositioned the gun, and fired off a long continuous volley – DUH, DUH, DUH, DUH, DUH, DUH, DUH, DUH...

With only three of them, Wade knew they were hopelessly outgunned. He snatched up the handset of the landline. "Six, this is four over! Six, this is four over!" he yelled over the deafening rattle of the PKM.

"This is six, go," replied Lieutenant Testenkov.

"We're going to be overrun!" Wade shouted into the handset. Then he ducked just in time to avoid getting cut down by an enfilade of bullets. He grabbed his walkabout and yelled for Oleksandr and Danylo, but got no reply. Hearing the gun battle, the two flew out of the barracks and ran to the sound of the guns.

The machine gun jackhammered violently – DUH, DUH, DUH, DUH, DUH, DUH... The tracers raked the bushes and base of trees, the deafening noise reverberated off the apartment complexes. The fluted barrel of Ivan's PKM glowed red hot. The burst of fire dropped two of Kerlikowski's men and pinned down the rest who took cover along a line of trees. They were now a scant fifty-meters away, and right outside the barracks. A minute later, Testenkov marshaled the rest of his platoon to get them out to the fight. With about ten men behind him, the young officer led the way out of the barracks and into a hail of bullets, getting caught in a murderous crossfire. Wade had a front-row seat, watching them all get mercilessly cut down. A few soldiers, who didn't run outside, fired from the windows at the separatists who returned fire, peppering the buildings' façade with a torrent of bullets and RPGs.

Wade stopped to reload his AK, and suddenly realized blood was running down his neck. Believing he'd been shot, he sat down his rifle, and with both hands, he quickly pat down his head and neck, checking if he still had a head. It was only a graze. Glancing over to his right, he saw Bogdan's body slumped down in the trench, his face was a mass of shredded flesh. He realized he was wearing Bogdan's blood. Wade shook it off, put on his helmet, and got back into the fight. He aimed his rifle – B-B-B-BRRAAAAAAW! B-B-B-BRRAAAAAAW!

Ivan fired off another long burst, emptying the 250-round ammo box. Grabbing another one, he loaded it and continued hammering away – DUH, DUH, DUH…. DUH, DUH, DUH… slowing down his rate of fire.

"Why do they always attack on our shift?!" yelled Ivan.

It soon became an orgy of chaos, as one could hardly tell who was firing at who, and from where.

On the slagheap, about a thousand-meters to the north of the gun battle erupting at the trench line, Gorgan slammed another shell into the chamber of his Lapua and squeezed off a shot – WHRACCK! A second later, his bullet ripped out Ivan's throat, dropping him into the trench.

"Nice shot," said Vadim. "You closed him out!"

Noting the direction of the shot, Wade scowled as he discovered Ivan's body lying on the floor of the trench in a pool of blood. Wade realized he was now the only man defending the outpost of Ukrainian sovereign soil. He knew he had to get out.

To his right, he saw the first enemy fighter enter the trench. He was close enough for Wade to make out the black and orange ribbon of St. George on his kit. Wade turned and, with a savage growl, fired a long burst – B-B-B-BRRAAAAAAW, catapulting him back into the bottom of the trench. Then he pulled himself up and over the side of the earthen wall, taking one last glance at Ivan and Bogdan's bodies lying in the bottom of the trench. "Bastards!" he yelled, as he took off as fast as he could through the trees. Running pell-mell, he ran into Oleksandr and Danylo, who were firing at the separatists and had by now gained the trench. "Don't shoot! Don't shoot!" Wade shouted, as Oleksandr took aim at him.

Wade dove to the ground next to them. His heart slammed against his ribs. He gulped at the air, trying to slow his breathing enough to speak.

"Ivan and Bogdan?" yelled Oleksandr.
Wade shook his head.

What about the platoon?" asked Oleksandr.
 Wade shook his head again with a look of absolute disgust.

"Sonofabitch! What do we do now?!" roared Oleksandr in a seething rage.

"How many mags do you have?" asked Wade.

"I've got four," said Oleksandr, as machine-gun fire pulverized the ground in front of them, pelting them with a shower of dirt.

"That's Ivan's PKM they're firing. Sonofabitch!"

"Danylo?" yelled Wade.

"Bastards just got him" said Oleksandr, rolling Danylo's lifeless body to the side. A bullet struck him in the temple.

"And you've been hit too!"

"It's a graze. The rest is Bogdan's blood."

"Sonofabitch!" shouted Oleksandr.

WHRACCK! – Another sniper's bullet cracked overhead.

"Whoever that is, he's pinning down our guys in the next strongpoint," said Wade.

Another long burst of fire came from the trench line, ripping into the tree trunk Wade and the others were hiding behind. Another RPG exploded, sending a sheet of dirt over them. Wade could see more than a dozen rebels occupying the trench line. They let out a victory shout – "YAHHHH! YAHHHH!"

"Those bastards are celebrating," said Oleksandr, as he pulled some magazines off Danylo's kit. Then, adding insult to injury, the victors pulled down the tattered Ukrainian flag. And in a ceremonial gesture, they broke its wooden makeshift staff, and threw the flag to the ground, drawing out another victory cheer – "YAHHHH!"

"Don't celebrate too early, you fools," said Wade. "They'll be on top of us soon. We've got to fall back to the city council building. Follow me!"

As they got up to run – THWACK! THWACK! Bullets began to crack and hiss around them. Wade ran out front, with Oleksandr a few paces behind him.

"If we can just hole-up at the city council building, we might survive long enough for the cavalry to arrive," said Wade. "Okay? Let's go!"

Wade took one last glance at the trench. "Sergeant Kravets," he said, shaking his head, "you were always a stickler for your schedule."

Два

Alonso had been asleep for a few hours when the door of the bedroom opened. "Spaniard!"

"Get up!" said a man at the door as he turned on the lights.

"Qué demonios!" Alonso squinted his eyes to see who it was.

"My name is Lev. Get dressed quickly and come with me."

"Who are you? What do you want?"

"I'm with the militia. I'm sure Wade told you about me."

"Come on!" yelled Lev, waving his arm.

Jumping out of bed, Alonso raced to throw on his clothes and boots. He kissed Zlata, "I'll be back for you my sweet."

He looked back to see her waving goodbye. Running out to Lev's car, he could hear the sound of distant gunfire and explosions coming from the south. Then it dawned on him, he was missing a battle! He jumped in the back seat as Lev drove off. A man in the front seat handed him an AK. "It's loaded. Here are two mags. I'm Olek."

"What's our plan?" asked Alonso.

"To get into the fight," said Lev, as the car flew down the road toward the sound of the guns. Crossing over the railroad bridge, they could hear the battle getting closer. The road forked ahead, one way went high to a slagheap, the other descended into the valley below. As the car turned south and approached Zolote 4, the crack and hiss of bullets began to impact on the road just in front of the hood. One struck the front tire, causing Lev to jerk the wheel, launching the car into a deep ditch. "Get out!" exclaimed Lev.

Alonso went to grab the man in the front seat, who remained sedentary. "Leave him. He's dead!" yelled Olek.

The three of them dove into the ditch for cover as the car was being peppered with bullets. The windshield was blood-spattered and shot up.

"It's coming from the slagheap!" yelled Lev.

"We'll use the ditch to get out of here!" he added.

Leading the way, Lev ran east along the ditch until he reached a point where a field met an intersection, then he dove into the prone.

"Okay. He can't hit us at all," said Lev, trying to catch his breath.

"What are you saying?" asked Alonso.

"We run across the road here and into the woods."

"Okay, let's do this," agreed Alonso. Before he could say this, Lev had already started bolting across the road. As Alonso sprinted through the open space, he heard a single shot ring out. Reaching the edge of the woods, he dove into the bushes, and instinctively brushed himself to see if he'd been hit.

"He got Olek," said Lev.

Alonso parted some branches to see Olek lying face down in the road. He'd been shot in the chest.

"That was at least a five-hundred meter shot!" yelled Alonso.

"Not sure if we'll ever make it, but let's go," said Lev. The two got up and ran through the woods for Lev's house. From there they could plan their next move.

Три

Vrilnik and his men could hear the attack. They were about four kilometers west of the strong point. The partisan commander smiled in anticipation and made a last-minute check of the ambush line. Out to his front was a clear killing field. From the edge of the woodline to the "X" of the ambush was just over a hundred meters. On the flanks of his line, he placed his RPG gunners. They would take out the lead and trail vehicles respectively. In between, and about a meter or two apart, he positioned his twenty-three riflemen. Armed with AKs, they would lay down a wall of lead upon the commencement of the ambush. Then on both flanks, collocated with the RPGs, he placed his PKMs. On both sides of the road, which ran from Popasna to Zolote, was a low-lying ditch. It seemed a near perfect kill zone. When he felt satisfied, he came back to his position next to his far-right RPG-29 gunner and waited.

Moments later, the sound of several trucks could be heard streaming toward their position. Vrilnik's radio squelched as his security position called in. "Kraz Cobra in the lead, followed by three Kozak-2s."

Seconds later, Vrilnik saw the lead vehicle, it was a Kraz Cobra fighting vehicle. When it reached his predetermined point, he yelled "FIRE!" A second later, the fwoosh of the RPG's rocket slammed square into the side of the lead vehicle. It was Captain Volokh's truck. KABOOM! A column of flame erupted from the truck's cab like a giant blow torch, instantly roasting the driver alive. The rocket's impact unleashed a hellacious wall of bullets from the concealed position.

FWOOSH! KABOOM! Two more rockets fired, scoring direct hits on the trail vehicle. At the same time, the PKMs opened up – DUH, DUH, DUH, DUH, DUH, DUH, DUH...... the shower of bullets raked the side of the convoy; the tracers sparked against the metal hulks, launching fragments and ricochets – DUH, DUH, DUH, DUH, DUH, DUH, DUH, DUH...

Falling out of the truck's cab, in flames, Captain Volokh stood up long enough to face his attackers, screaming and wildly firing his rifle. He managed to fire several bursts until he was mercilessly cut down. He dropped face-first and was immolated like a human candle.

By this time, the second truck, which was the only mobile vehicle left in the convoy, began to move. Turning toward the woodline, the driver negotiated the low ditch, looking for a way out of the kill zone. Jockeying the truck like a camel, the top gunner returned fire with his 12.7-millimeter heavy machine gun – DOOH, DOOH, DOOH, DOOH....

Walking his tracers into the woodline, the gunner's heavy fire cut down a few separatists. Then, the truck stopped and disgorged five soldiers who dove to the prone and began returning fire. It had no sooner come to a stop when an RPG-7 fired from the woodline – FWOOSH! KABOOM! Hitting the turret. The warhead sent up a ball of flame, pelted the side of the truck with shrapnel, and dropped two men who had just climbed out of the back. Sergeant Kravets fell out of the passenger door and was somehow able to avoid getting himself decimated by the hellacious fire. He looked up to see the gunner slumped over in the turret, his body aflame.

Having watched Captain Volokh get burned alive, Sergeant Kravets took stock of the situation. From what he could tell, he now had about three men with him who were not dead. To make matters worse, he was in the middle of the kill zone and was pinned down with only the hulk of his truck as cover. The separatists' PKM continued to fire barbarously – DUH, DUH, DUH… DUH, DUH, DUH…

With the Ukrainian quick reaction force all but destroyed, Vrilnik now considered his next move; he decided to move his force on to Zolote. He picked up his radio: "Volk 2, this is Volk 3, over. Volk 2, this is Volk 3, over."

"Go ahead Volk 3," came the message from Marko through static.

"Convoy destroyed. Moving to your position now," said Vrilnik.

"Roger. Come with all haste! We're going after the city council building!" exclaimed Marko.

"Roger."

Leaving the dead and dying to their fate, Vrilnik's force ran to the panel vans and drove pell-mell toward Zolote.

Четыре

It was now just after seven in the morning. Pavel was rocked out of bed by the nearby gun battle that raged down the street. The intensity of the firefight made him think it was just outside the door. Hastily throwing on his pants and boots, he walked out in the living room to see Vasyli on the phone. Sitting down on the couch, he was fully dressed, wearing a military ball cap and load-bearing vest with ammo. By his side was his old Mosin–Nagant rifle.

"This is it. Bring every man you can, and meet me at the garage," said Vasyli, as he put away his phone.

"What's going on?" asked Pavel.

"We're under attack! I think the Russians are really going to advance over the border this time."

"Where are you going?"

"I'm going to war, son.... Come with me."

"You're going to get yourself killed. The army will..."

"The army is getting overrun! That noise you heard... that's the sound of the army getting beat!" yelled Vasyli.

"It's time to get off the fence!"

Vasyli ran out of the apartment and down the stairs.

"Wait!" said Pavel, as he flew down the stairs on his heels. "Wait!"

Vasyli ran out of the front door and didn't get but a few steps outside the apartment when a shot rang out – WHRACCK! knocking him to the ground. The accuracy of the Lapua sniper rifle proved its worth at three-thousand feet per second. The piercing report of the precision weapon reverberated throughout the quad of buildings. Looking out of the door and onto the horizon, Pavel judged the shot to have originated from the slagheap, about a full kilometer away. Pavel sprinted out and grabbed Vasyli's body and dragged him back into the lobby of the complex and closed the door.

Vasyli's chest heaved in pain as he gasped for breath. Pavel looked at the entry wound; it was mid-chest. Blood pooled on Vasyli's jacket as his light green smock grew ever darker with each heartbeat. Making a terrible hissing sound as he inhaled, Vasyli clinched his old rifle. The commotion led Yelizaveta to run downstairs. She screamed as she saw the old man on his back. She sat on the floor and put his head in her lap.

Then looking up at Pavel, Vasyli smiled and said, "Son, live your life.... Stop living in the past."

"It's okay, father. Don't talk," said Pavel.

Vasyli's breathing became increasingly laborious. As he inhaled, his breath sucked through a hole in his chest. In the realization that he was on the verge of eternity, Vasyli said, "son, Stepan isn't real." Yelizaveta nodded in collaboration.

The words hit Pavel hard as steel. "What are you talking about?" he exclaimed, watching the pink foam rise from Vasyli's nose and mouth.

"You don't want... to hear the truth... you don't want your illusions destroyed," said Vasyli.

"How could you say that?" asked Pavel, shaking his head in utter disbelief.

"Don't you see? Your mind created him... because you needed him," said Vasyli, coughing up blood.

"Live your life, my son," he said as he breathed his last.

Pavel looked over at Yelizaveta, who nodded slowly. Pavel looked down at his father; rage filled every cell of his being as a single tear ran down his face. Then, as he closed his father's eyes, Pavel's face turned to stone. He nodded, as if accepting this was all somehow preordained. Then, in one fluid motion, he snatched up Vasyli's rifle and blood-soaked vest of ammo. He put it on and stood up. He pulled back on the rifle's bolt, checking its status. Without a word, he bolted out of the apartment complex and, despite his wife's pleas, he ran to the sound of the guns.

Пять

Having gained the strong point, the combined separatist force maneuvered through Zolote 4, up to the city council building. As they did, a few Ukrainian soldiers ran out of the barracks and began to engage the rebels, but were quickly outgunned. Rebel heavy machine guns laid down a withering curtain of lead, shredding the front of the barracks and taking out six soldiers at once. Two other soldiers jumped in a car and attempted to drive off. A second later, they found themselves in a seething inferno when an RPG smashed into the car's windshield. The deafening explosion sent pieces of shrapnel ripping through the air. The separatists then fanned out around the city council building like wolves plunging amongst sheep, covering the front and sides.

Approaching Zolote 4 on foot, Lev and Alonso could hear the report of the guns. Running south, they could see the separatists poised to attack the council building. With Lev in the lead, they ran across a small field between two houses, somehow undetected. As Lev broke the corner of his house, he was almost dropped by Wade, who had taken up a position outside Lev's garage.

"Don't shoot! Don't shoot!"

"Stay down," yelled Wade. "This place is crawling with separatists," he said, pointing toward the council building.

"Alonso! Glad you could make it!" exclaimed Wade.

"Did you leave us any beer?" joked Oleksandr.

"Here, follow me inside," said Lev, opening his front door.

As they ran inside, a few beer bottles got kicked around. The house was in disarray and smelled like mildew.

With a look of 'yeah, I know,' Lev nodded his head, "I'll have the maid clean up."

While the men took up defensive positions at the doors and windows, Lev took stock of their situation. "One, two, three, four, five, six of us, versus all of them."

"Great odds," said Alonso, "and yes, there are plenty of beers left."

"Where's Danylo, Ivan, and Bogdan?" asked Alonso.

Wade shook his head.

In the distance, they could hear the triumphant separatists celebrate the capture of the council building. Inside, Marko's men took several OSCE hostages, consolidating them into one room.

"We heard the fighting. What's the situation? Is this World War III?" asked Lev.

"I'm not a hundred percent sure," said Wade.

A knock was heard at the door. "See who it is," directed Lev.

"It's Pavel," said Wade, opening the door, nodding in approval.

"Come in," said Lev, looking Pavel over.

"Old bolt-action, huh?"

"Here, take this," said Wade, handing him an AK-47.

"It's hot," he added.

"Here," said Lev, handing him two loaded magazines.

"Okay, the main force should be here in ten minutes. When these turds try to run back to the line, we'll light them up. Make sense?"

The city council building was a mere three-hundred meters away. Shouts of victory could be heard coming out of the building, as the Phantom Battalion celebrated their victory.

"What about your company, Wade?" asked Lev.

"Decimated."

"When?"

"Got a call from Sergeant Kravets on the way here. There are maybe three of them left alive," said Wade, glancing at his watch, "about ten minutes ago."

Another knock came at the door.

"It's Fyodor," said Pavel.

"Come in, join the party," invited Wade.

"What's the plan?" asked Fyodor.

"Okay American, what's next?" asked Lev.

"Well, if Captain Volokh had radioed headquarters, then we can expect a quick reaction force within another ten minutes or so."

"What do you see?" asked Wade.

"Okay, I got one guy outside in the prone with a belt fed, looks like two... no, three panel vans around back... then, on the second floor, I can make out several gun barrels."

Just as another round of victory celebration was underway, the Ukrainian Army arrived. North of the council building, three armored 6x6 vehicles rolled to a stop. Pavel looked out a window to see the gold and sky blue Ukrainian flag flying atop one of the 6x6 vehicles. His chest swelled with patriotic pride.

Immediately, an eruption of fire poured out of the building on the convoy – B-B-B-BRRAAAAAAW! B-B-B-BRRAAAAAAW!

The Ukrainian convoy returned fire – DUH, DUH, DUH... DUH, DUH, DUH...

Bullets whipped through every window, gouging chunks from the masonry, shredding the walls apart. The men inside flew to the ground, or were cut down by the heavy machine guns. A few separatists tried to run out, but were decimated.

To the east, about five-hundred meters away, Vadim and Gorgan had an elevated view of the gun battle. From the slagheap, they watched the whole ordeal unfold.

"Just like Odessa," said Gorgan, laconically.

"Yes. Blood and fire," agreed Vadim.

Back at Lev's house, Wade and the survivors watched things unfold, making everyone antsy. They could hear the crackle and pop of the guns, along with the faint cries and moans of those inside.

"Should we go out?" asked Oleksandr.

"No, wait!" yelled Lev. "Those guys in those 6x6s will mistake us for separatists."

"Yeah, let's wait. Their fries are done," said Wade, watching black smoke billow out of the windows. Outside, several burned-out cars were smoldering on the road.

"This isn't over," said Fyodor.

"What do you mean?" asked Wade.

"You have to kill the wolf," said Fyodor, in a solemn tone.

"Where is he?" asked Pavel.

"The slagheap."

"That's where we took fire. He blasted Ivan and flushed us out of the trench line," said Wade.

"I'm going. Who's coming with me?" roused Pavel.

"Let's go!" shouted Fyodor.

"Where are you going?" asked Lev.

"To kill the bastard who killed my father."

"And Ivan!" added Wade.

"Let's hunt him down like the dog he is. After all, there's no hunting like the hunting of man. Pavel, we're coming with you," said Wade, counting Oleksandr and Alonso.

"Alright, let's go!" exclaimed Lev.

Leading the way, Fyodor ran east out of Lev's house, while the others followed closely behind. With the slagheap out on the horizon, they ran along the backside of several buildings. Then, using a barn as cover, they sprinted across a field toward the railway tracks. As they got closer, they watched Vadim's black sedan sped off north down the trail.

"He's heading for the mine," declared Fyodor.

As they crested the tracks, Vadim's car could be seen driving north along the winding trail. About a hundred meters away, they paused to take several shots at it, blasting a tire.

"I hit it," said Oleksandr.

"Light it up," said Wade.

They let out a volley of lead, bringing the car to a sudden halt as it slumped into a shallow ditch. Pavel and the others continued to fire pot-shots as Vadim and Gorgan bailed out into the ditch. As Pavel and the others closed on the car, Vadim and Gorgan got up and run along a hedgerow up the hill.

"One of them is running west!" yelled Lev.

"That's not Vadim," said Fyodor. "Let him go. It's Vadim you want."

The four men paused to take several more shots at Gorgan, but he soon disappeared behind the slope of the hill.

15

In the Mine

"Do you see it?" asked Fyodor, pointing to the open-pit mine. The five men ran up the side of the hill from which the mine was cut. Reaching the mouth of the mine first, Fyodor looked back with a grin. The others were right on his heels. "Slava Ukraini!" exclaimed Fyodor, with a look of triumphant confidence.

"Slava Ukraini! Heroiam slava," replied Pavel, in a martial tone with a sense of elation. Fyodor ran up the steps of the mine entrance, opened the door, and walked in. As he did, he was met with a hail of gunfire that nearly ripped him in half. Hearing the eruption of fire, Wade stopped short of going through the door. The others fell into the prone. The sound of the gunfire reverberated out of the door. Gasping a deep sigh of pain, Fyodor looked back at Pavel, and in a faint whisper, intoned the words, "Slava Ukraini!" Then, with a smile of relief, like a great weight had fallen away, he fell down on the steps and breathed a final sigh; his eyes staring in death.

"Fyodor!" yelled Pavel.

"He's gone. I saw him go down," said Wade, slumping down on the side of the hill, struggling to catch his breath.

"That's certain death in there, my friend. Let's wait him out," said Wade, noticing the intense throbbing sensation in his arm. He'd been nicked in his right bicep and couldn't move his arm without excruciating pain.

"I'm not letting him get away," said Pavel, as he stood and walked toward the mine entrance.

"I'd go with you, but my gun arm's shot," said Wade, looking at Lev, Oleksandr, and Alonso, who showed no desire of going into what appeared to be certain death.

"Just don't let him come out alive!" demanded Pavel.

"He won't get past us," promised Lev, as he watched Pavel give the sign of the cross.

"God go with you," prayed Wade.

Pavel nodded, then walked up the steps of the entrance with his rifle at the ready. He was met by a wall of stale air and noxious gas. He breathed it in, tasting its sour tang. Stepping through the doorway, he saw what was left of Fyodor; his face was barely recognizable. He walked down the steps and ventured slowly into the darkness of the mineshaft. Walking softly, further and further into the blackness, he could feel the perspiration began to pool on his lower back. Beads of sweat ran down his face. "Where are you, you bastard," he thought.

About ten-meters in, he paused to let his eyes adjust to the pitch blackness. He stood as still as a statue. He heard the creaking of timber, and the sound of water dripping onto rocks. He took in a deep breath and felt the grit of coal dust on his teeth. His goal was to wait a full five minutes to acclimate. But the question was, would he have that long?

Standing in the pitch blackness, Pavel worried if he would ever see his darling Yelizaveta again. How he longed to make things right with her. But, would he have a chance? Fear gripped him. Yet, his desire for vengeance triumphed. Pavel intoned the words "Kuriye Iesu Christeh Elehson meh." He said it three times in his mind and could sense a settled calmness descend upon him. "God bless you, priest," he thought, "What a gift to the body you are."

He looked down at the rifle, and mused how comfortable it felt in his hands. He was surprised to see the situation that he now found himself in. Then he thought, "It's not vengeance I seek. No. Lord, that's Your purview. Nonetheless, I know that You will decide who dies in the next few minutes."

Gradually, his eyes began to detect more details. He could make out more of the walls, then the floor, then a post. Satisfied by the silence, he decided to keep moving. Proceeding at a slow pace, he concentrated on controlling his breathing and setting down each step with care. Cognizant of the sound of his shoes, he concentrated on muffling his steps, slowly allowing them to fall. He touched the weapon with his left hand, and checking the position of the safety, he made sure it was on "fire."

With his eyes adjusted, he could now see about ten meters in front of him. He could feel the walls of the mineshaft closing in. The ceiling was getting lower. Walking at a crouch, he felt a strain in his back. Then about a hundred meters in, he caught the pungent stench of death. The smell of death was so strong that it masked the fumes of methane gas. He had smelled this before. It was the stench of rotting human flesh. "Three days, by the smell of it," he thought.

The rancid stench filled his nostrils. He stopped and instinctively covered his nose and mouth with his shirt. He began to think about his father, about how he had failed to say goodbye. He thought about the war; "Had the Russians advanced along the line? Was his family safe?"

Before he could go further down the rabbit hole of introspection, he heard footsteps out in front of him. He stopped, taking cover behind a wooden post that stood in the middle of the shaft, then leveled his AK-47. He determined by the sound of the steps that they were no more than thirty-meters ahead. As it turned out, Vadim found the shaft collapsed at about the midway point, no doubt from the tremendous barrage of mortars. Having hit a dead end, he was now coming back. The footsteps were getting closer and closer. Pavel could not tell for certain how far away the steps were, but they were getting closer.

Pavel broke the silence, "Is that you, Zimri?" he voiced in a tone as cold as an executioner.

Vadim instinctively flipped on his flashlight toward the voice and fired a deafening five-round blast with his AK – B-B-B-B-BRRAAAAAAW! The bullets ricocheted, bouncing off the rockface of the shaft. He swung his flashlight in Pavel's direction, then fired again – B-B-B-B-B-B-B-B-BRRAAAAAAW!

"Every profound spirit needs a mask," said Pavel, "and you certainly wore yours well."

"What are you mumbling?" asked Vadim. "Why doesn't the hero come out and show himself?"

"I saw you before, only I didn't recognize you," said Pavel, looking down to see the face of a young miner, shot execution-style. "But I certainly recognize your work."

Vadim fired a long continuous burst until the bolt of the rifle clanked to a stop. The inside of the mineshaft reverberated with the thunderous noise. Then Pavel heard more footsteps as Vadim closed the distance. He was getting closer, now perhaps twenty-meters away.

"Do you know what the boy said?" asked Vadim, in a slow and solemn tone.

Pavel offered no response, but wanted to know just the same.

"He merely stated, 'I'm not yet dead,'" revealed Vadim.

"Not yet dead! Is that all?" thought Pavel.

But then the words hit him like a locomotive. Pavel found the words to be pregnant with meaning. It was as if the Afghan boy had said, "is that the best you can do," or "death is not the end, yet only an entrance into glory," or something to that effect.

Vadim no doubt had uttered these words to injure him, yet for Pavel, the words had the reverse effect. They gave him a sense of relief at the revelation. He felt as though an old cancerous cyst had been cut out and now dropped free from his soul. Processing it all, Pavel said, "I'm not tormented by that anymore... besides, I find the boy's words to be remarkably patriotic! I too, am not yet dead, and neither is my Country!"

"Hmph, I should have killed you when I had the chance," said Vadim.

"Who's to say you could've? My steps, as well as my days, are all numbered," replied Pavel.

"Just what the world needs, another fanatic!" said Vadim, as he took a cigar out of his pocket and lit it. As he struck the match, the glow illuminated his face. Instinctively, Pavel raised his rifle to his shoulder, and in an instant, fired three rounds in rapid succession – BRAHT, BRAHT, BRAHT! The third bullet hit Vadim in the chest. Gasping for breath, he dropped his rifle to the floor of the mine.

Something told Pavel to run out of the mine. He turned and ran as hard as he could, knocking his head on the low roof of the mine. He grunted in pain. Vadim breathed out a mouthful of cigar smoke, "blood and fire," said Vadim, then let the lit match fall free from his hand.

The match hit the floor of the shaft, igniting the methane fumes, touching off a sheet of flame. Pavel was a few steps from the entrance. With a growing combustion behind him lighting his way, Pavel dove out of the mine's entrance. A terrifying rumble grew from the bowels of the shaft. Then with a shriek like that of a hundred demons, the mine exploded with blinding white light. In the deafening blast, a plume of smoke and coal dust shot out of the mouth of the open pit, engulfing the whole enclosure into flames.

Два

It was Sunday morning. Pavel awoke and became aware of his surroundings. He was in a hospital bed, and discovered his arms covered in gauze. He sensed a throbbing pain in his arms, as the drugs he'd been given began to wear off. He glanced up to see a slow dripping IV bag and other assorted beeping equipment, of which he neither knew name nor function. Outside, he could hear birds chirping, welcoming the new day. The walls were characteristically bland, except for a few framed prints, one of which was Kuindzhi's *Red Sunset on the Dnieper*.

"Hello! Anyone there?" he summoned, searching the room for a nurse or orderly.

"Hello!" he shouted, sensing the antiseptic odor of alcohol swabs in his nose.

"Good morning," greeted a nurse. "How was your sleep?"

"Good... I think. How long have I been here?"

"Since yesterday."

Pavel raised his arm. "What happened here?"

"Your arms were burned, but not too badly. I suspect you'll be discharged today."

"That's very good. Nurse, how did I get here?"

"The army," she replied.

"Can I get some food?"

"Yes. Lunch will be out in an hour, but you can have some juice now. Would you like that?"

"Yes, thank you."

Before the nurse could come back with a drink, Pavel had fallen back asleep. When he woke up again, he saw his friend Anton.

"Have a drink. The nurse is gone," said Anton, holding out a flask of vodka.

"No thanks," he said, taking a sniff and grunting as he worked to sit up on the gurney. "What happened?"

"You got blown up in the mine."

"I mean, what happened in town?"

"The separatists captured the city council building and ambushed an army convoy outside of town. There was a lot of carnage, but..."

"What about the Russians?" asked Pavel.

"What about them?" shrugged Anton.

"They're still massing on the border, like always."

"I see."

"From my house, I had a front-row seat for the whole thing," said Anton. "The army arrived and surrounded the separatists as they tried to barricade themselves inside; it's just like they've done in the past. It looked like they were trying to retake the town. However, then the army showed up and surrounded the building, calling for them to surrender."

"Then what happened?" prodded Pavel, testing his pain threshold by bending his arms.

"Well, then the separatists opened fire and the army gave them hell. I'm sorry to say, the building went up in flames. And after the Army finished annihilating those at the city council, they moved down to the trench line, and retook the strong points that had fallen to the LPR."

"I can't help but think this is strangely like the dream I had last night," said Pavel.

"Really?"

"I was standing in a field. It was full and immense. I laid down with my head to the ground. A sound rose out of the soil, like a million hoof beats. The grass was high and soft, and swayed gently with the breeze. I looked out as far as I could see. I walked east, till I came to the bank of a mighty river. On the other side of the river, I watched the grass of the steppe as it became lost to a remorseless flame. I was sad to see the waves of grass consumed, leaving the earth scorched beneath. But no sooner had the grass died, than it sprouted to life again. Then I crossed the raging blue torrent, reached the other side, and walked in the grass that had become high and soft, and swayed in the gentle breeze."

"I, for one, hope that your dream is prescient," said Anton.

Pavel's thoughts went to Lev, Wade, and the others with him. "My friend, I'm sorry about your son," said Pavel.

"Fyodor was a soldier. He did his duty," said Anton.

"He died well," assured Pavel. "In fact, without him, my father would never have been avenged."

The sterile nature of what he said bothered him. He hadn't any time yet to mourn his father's loss. Anton beat him to it.

"Someday I'll mourn his loss, but for now, I choose to celebrate his sacrifice."

"Well said, sir. I'll do the same," said Pavel.

Just then, Pavel's wife and daughters entered the room.

"Sweetheart," said Yelizaveta, looking for a way to hug him. His face grimaced as he reached out and gave her a big hug.

"I love you, my sweet," he said, watching her eyes well with tears as she returned the 'I love you.'

"Papa," said Tatyana, putting her arms around him.

Pavel's heart rejoiced at the sight of his family. Savka walked in with his granddaughter. "I love you grandpa," she said, melting Pavel's heart.

The nurse returned and sat a cup of juice on his bed tray.

"Mr. Koval," said the nurse, "this is Dr. Melnyk. He's here to talk with you about your injuries."

"Hello Mr. Koval," greeted Dr. Melnyk.

"Hello," said Pavel.

"How are you feeling?"

"Not too bad. Were it not for my arms, I'd be great."

"Okay, so regarding your injuries, you have second-degree burns on both arms, one on your neck here, and your cheek. There will be some swelling and blisters, and you'll probably have some scarring as well. Just to be on the safe side, I'm going to have you stay overnight," said Dr. Melnyk.

"Okay, if that's absolutely necessary," said Pavel, noticeably irritated.

"You've been through a lot. I just want to watch you for a night. Is that okay?" asked Dr. Melnyk.

"Okay."

Soon after, Pavel's lunch arrived, then he spent a little more time with his family. When he got tired again, they let him go back to sleep.

Три

It was now late Sunday night. While Pavel slept in the hospital, Savka and Wade were talking on the steps of the family's apartment complex. Wade sat across from Savka with his arm in a makeshift sling. He was a mess. As he hunched forward, the pain was visible on his face. She looked him over. Dried blood was splattered all over his digitized multicam jacket. She reached over and picked off some unknown piece of debris from his beard.

"When will the war be over for you?" she asked.

"I don't know. That all depends..."

"Depends on what?"

"It's late, but before I go, I want to ask you something," said Wade.

"Okay," said Savka.

"I've lived a crazy life up to this point, the next logical step would be to marry a Ukrainian woman," he said with a wide grin.

She laughed and playfully slapped his face.

"Does that mean yes?" he said.

"Of course," she replied, leaning in for another kiss. A slow grin spread itself across Wade's face. He leaned over and drew her to himself with his good arm. Holding the kiss for a long moment, he took in the warmth of her touch.

"I'll need to ask your father," said Wade.

"Why? I already said yes."

"I know, but that's just how things are normally done. I just want to do things right."

"You mean, do things religiously?" she asked, adding a sour note to the word.

"I suppose," he said, searching for a fuller reply.

"Hmm, religions. They do as much harm as they do good," she said.

"What do you mean?" he asked in a laconic tone, wounded at the dismissiveness of her words.

"You think a man's creed hinders his intellect?" he added.

"No. I'm just tired of seeing people sanctioning their murder with religion."

"On that, we fully agree. It seems to me, God tires of being called down to sanction political causes."

"But you do believe in God, don't you?" he asked with bated breath.

"I do," she said with a nod. "I just prefer to keep my thoughts on those sorts of things to myself, that's all."

"Do you know anything about Ukrainian wedding ceremonies?" she asked.

"A little. I've seen the Deer Hunter."

"What?"

"Never mind. Enlighten me... but do you think your parents will accept me?"

"My mother will love you."

"But will your father?"

"Only time will tell," she said with a playful smile.

"What do you mean?"

"Just trust me," she said, as she leaned in for another kiss.

Четыре

Pavel woke from deep sleep. It was just after dark. He was sweating profusely, and his arms were throbbing with intense pain. His hospital room was dark. Then, the door of his room slowly opened. From the light in the hallway he could see a man walk in, but couldn't quite tell who it was. The man closed the distance from the door and was at his bedside. It was the waiter from the *Bell Ringer*.

"Pavel. My name is Oleksiy. I've got to get you out of here."

"What do you mean? Why?"

"Trust me. You're in danger. The good doctor... isn't. I'm with the SBU.[1] The doctor is part of an antigovernment clandestine network operating here in Zolote, and Hirske. We've been tracking his movements for a while. We can't quite put our finger on how he's doing it, but we know he's up to no good."

"What are you saying?"

"If you stay here, you're going to die," said Oleksiy, handing him a pair of pants.

"Really? Why would anyone want to..." said Pavel, stopping as he heard footsteps in the hallway.

"They know you're with the militia. Come with me. We're getting out of here," he said, opening the window.

Pavel sat up as far as he could, then was pulled out of the bed by Oleksiy. He pulled off his patient gown and threw on the pants, which were a little snug. He staggered toward the window to find the top of a ladder.

"You have to climb down," said Oleksiy, as he helped Pavel through the window. Pavel stepped down and nearly fell two stories as his foot missed a rung, causing the aluminum frame of the ladder to clang.

"Hurry," he said.

Pavel labored to get to the base of the ladder without killing himself. Stepping off the last rung, he was met by Lev and some other members of the militia.

"Wow, you really got banged up!" said Lev, looking over his wounds. Pavel looked up at the hospital room.

---

[1] Security Service of Ukraine (SBU).

"Don't worry. We'll take care of the doctor. We're going to send him off the planet. Let's get you home."

16

The Wedding

Nothing about the Donbas had changed. Despite the terrible week's bloodletting, things returned as they were. Once the dust settled, both sides returned to their entrenchments, and peace remained elusive. Nonetheless, a measure of peace came to Pavel and his family, albeit at a price.

It was Saturday morning. Two weeks had passed since Grandpa Vasyli's death. The town of Zolote buried all its dead and picked up the pieces of their lives, making the best of things as they could. At the usual time, Pavel and Tatyana arrived at the butchery and got the shop ready for a busy day. As they did, Father Malashenko drove up and parked.

"Good morning, Father," said Pavel, greeting the priest as he stepped inside.

"Good morning, Pavel. How are your arms?"

"No worse for wear. The gauze came off last week, but there are a few spotty places left. I feel good nonetheless."

"And how is your wife?"

"At home baking cakes for tomorrow."

"And your new apprentice?"

"She's catching on very quickly. I believe I'll soon be able to stay at home," said Pavel.

"Ahem, not a chance," said Tatyana, loud enough to be heard as she continued her work in the back.

"How is life, my son?"

"By God's grace, it is very good... and I'll somehow survive my sister's visit!"

"Oh really? How long is she in town?"

"Thank the Lord for just two days! I was going to come over later today. You didn't have to trouble yourself."

"No trouble at all. After all, it was probably my turn to visit you. Besides, I've really missed our deep discussions."

"Me too, Father. Not everyone has a mind for theology... Alright, I have one for you, Father."

"Splendid."

"I've done a great deal of thinking since my father's funeral."

"I'm sure you have. Anything in particular?" asked Father Malashenko.

"Well, do you remember the part in *The Brothers Karamazov,* when Father Zossima bowed."

"Yes, certainly," replied the priest, listening intently.

"Well, I don't think I ever understood that until now."

"Okay Pavel, now I'm dying to know."

"Well, Father Zossima wasn't bowing to Dimitri Karamazov per se, rather, he was bowing to all human suffering."

"That's a great insight. I have read that book several times and never realized that. Do you mind if I use it? I'll cite you of course."

"Hah-hah. Don't worry. That one's free. You know, in all of our talks, I've yet to ask you one important question."

"What's that?" asked Father Malashenko.

"I've been wondering, how are you able to do what you do? What keeps you going?"

"I don't think I've ever been asked that before... Well, I suppose I've always aspired to be like Abraham's unnamed servant. Do you know who I mean?"

"I've forgotten."

"Do you have time for a longer answer?"

"Of course, Father. My assistant," said Pavel, looking in the back of the shop, "will take care of things."

"I heard that!" exclaimed Tatyana playfully.

"Okay. Well, as you know, Abraham found himself between a rock and a hard place. He was given a wondrous promise that God would make his descendants like the stars in the sky. Remarkably, this is all to happen through the son of promise, who is Isaac. Earlier, as you remember, Abraham got ahead of God with his own plan. But then he resigned himself to God's way. Then, he summoned his oldest servant, and in the light of God's promise, Abraham sends his chief servant back to Mesopotamia to acquire a wife for Isaac. If that's not remarkable enough, what's even more so is, what we know regarding Abraham's unnamed servant. He was truly a remarkable man of faith. Surely, he had the faith that could move mountains. He considered the fulfillment of his oath to be a matter of life and death. It was of the utmost importance to him that God's will be done."

"Excuse me," said Tatyana, as she brought out a basket full of items.

"These are for you, Father," said Pavel.

"Thank you so much! Well, I should be going..."

"Wait Father, please tell me the rest of the story," said Pavel.

"Yes, of course... And so, what is also remarkable is, the servant sought God's guidance and waited on God's providence to play out, and he did so in the everyday occurrences of life. That's what I think is the most remarkable thing about this servant. Do you see? He had no name. And so, he was the no-named servant of God. However, with a bit of sanctified imagination, I suspect it was none other than the Eliezer of Genesis chapter fifteen; he was Abraham's chief servant. If this is Eliezer, then his faith and service is even more amazing. Do you remember him from Genesis fifteen?"

"I've forgotten," said Pavel, "But I'm intrigued all the more."

"Well, because of Sarah's barrenness, Abraham had presumed to pass his great inheritance onto Eliezer, yet God reassured Abraham that it would be through Isaac that he would be blessed. My point is, if this no-named servant was indeed Eliezer, his reward was simply seeing God's will being done. For, consider, if the no-named servant had failed in his mission, he might have thought Abraham's inheritance would have passed to him."

"I see," said Pavel, "this no-named servant was truly selfless."

"Precisely. And when the unnamed servant saw God's plan unfolding, when Rebekah agreed to come back with him to be Isaac's bride, he saw God's will being done, and worshipped the Lord. And so, regarding this ambiguity of who this servant is, I believe it's most telling that this selfless servant of the Lord has no name. It's in this spirit that I serve the God of heaven."

"That's wonderful, Father! I too endeavor to serve God in this way! I love that! And I truly believe that you most certainly serve God in this manner!"

"Thank you, Pavel. If I ever did anything good, I don't believe it was me doing it!"

"You know Pavel, it just occurred to me..."

"What's that, Father?"

"This is rather strange I think..."

"What's that?"

"Well, in the course of two weeks, I have buried your father, God rest his soul, baptized your future son-in-law, and will tomorrow marry him to your daughter. That's quite a lot for one family!"

Два

It was the next day. The azure tiles on the roof of the Temple of St. George glistened brightly in the noonday sun. Outside, it was perfectly clear, as an August breeze carried choral melodies out of the windows of the church and into the surrounding fields. As the church bells sounded forth joyous tones, inside the sanctuary, a celebration of life was underway. A man and woman were to be joined in holy matrimony. Sitting on the front pew with his family, in living color, Pavel took in the tableau. Inside the church could be seen an explosion of color with the intricately painted icons and candles. The couple wore white embroidered Vyshyvankas, and Savka's hair was returned to its beautiful brown color, intricately braided and decorated with various flowers and ribbons.

For Pavel, the wedding celebration was a picture of beauty and strength. The sound of the choir rose in one massive wave of resonance, like a dark river, then crescendoed. Wade and Savka faced each other as Father Malashenko read to them the Holy Sacrament of Marriage. Holding candles, the couple stood over a beautiful red and white embroidered rushnyk, while attendants stood behind them both, holding crowns above their heads.

"A man of worth fears God, hates evil, and loves his family, friends, and countrymen, and is willing to make sacrifices for their well-being," said Father Malashenko, "even when it's not appreciated."

He went on, "The Book of Ruth is set in the time of the Judges, which was a dark period in Israel's history. It was a time when everyone did what was right in their own eyes. There was widespread idolatry, sexual immorality, and injustice. But even during those dark days, God was not without a faithful people. God had men such as Boaz, who was a man of moral worth. While there were so many commendable things about Boaz, perhaps the most was his desire to see things done right; his wish was to honor the law of God. There's no doubt that he loved Ruth, and wanted her to be his wife, but things had to be done right. This reminds us that, honoring God's Word honors God."

"My friends, we are gathered together today to join this Boaz to this Ruth."

The couple then put their hands on the Bible, as they recited their vows. The shadow of the cross passed over them as Father Malashenko intoned the words: "The servant of God, Thomas, is crowned for the servant of God, Savka, in the Name of the Father and of the Son and of the Holy Ghost. Amen. The servant of God, Savka, is crowned for the servant of God, Thomas, in the Name of the Father and of the Son and of the Holy Ghost. Amen."

Wade smiled at Savka, happy she had worn her cross. Led by Father Malashenko, the couple then walked around the altar three times, symbolizing their first steps as a married couple, and the covenant of marriage they had entered into, in the eyes of God. As the ceremony came to its end, the priest recited parting blessings upon the newlyweds. To the groom, Father Malashenko said: "Be thou magnified, O Bridegroom, as Abraham, and blessed as Isaac, and multiplied as Jacob. Walk in peace and work in righteousness, as the commandments of God."

Then to the bride, he said: "And thou O Bride, be thou magnified as Sarah, glad as Rebecca, and multiplied like unto Rachel, rejoicing in thine own husband, fulfilling the conditions of the law. For so it is well pleasing unto God." Then Father Malashenko, smiling with benevolence, finished the ancient ceremony intoning the words, "Na zisete!"[1]

Enraptured with the joyous moment, Pavel glanced at Yelizaveta. Her face began to flood with tears of joy.

"I thought I lost you," she said, sobbing.

Pavel lovingly touched the face that he knew by heart, mumbled a tearful apology, pulled her close, and kissed her with all the tenderness in him.

---

[1] May you live!

Три

The next day, Pavel and Yelizaveta hosted a traditional wedding after-party in their apartment. The wedding reception the day before, had gone well into the night. Filled to maximum capacity, their living room swelled with all his friends, including Vano, Kezia, and Ehzi. A hand-drawn banner was draped from wall to wall, with the words: "Congratulations on tying the knot!"

Pavel stood up with his glass held high. "My friends, I raise a toast, 'To the health of the newlyweds.'"

All the guests began to shout "Gorka, gorka, gorka,"[2] prompting Wade and Savka to kiss again, for what was probably the hundredth time of the day.

"You almost feel sorry for them having to kiss every time someone yells 'gorka' in a toast!" exclaimed Anton, prompting the couple to kiss again.

"Well, Pavel," said Anton, placing a brothering hand on his shoulder, "what are your plans now?"

Pavel took in the importance of the question. "Before, my only plan was to leave. Now, my only plan is to be a husband, a father, and a grandpa... oh, and I almost forgot... a butcher," he said, hugging Yelizaveta, who stood smiling nearby.

"Simple enough," said Anton.

"What about you, my friend?" asked Pavel.

"I suppose I'll keep mining, and perhaps one day I'll make an impact in a meaningful way."

---

[2] The wine is 'bitter,' and the couple must kiss for as long as possible to take out the bitter taste of the wine.

"May I share something I've learned lately?" asked Pavel.

"By all means."

"I have found that many wonder if they will ever make an impact in the world, but a veteran never has that problem," said Pavel.

"Thank you, Pavel," said Anton, "We've come a long way since we had to run the gauntlet of that infamous Salang Pass... three kilometers of hell... not to mention, we survived that day coming back from that village! What was its name?"

"Charbagh."

"That's it! How we ever lived through that is beyond me."

As Pavel listened to Anton, he was surprised to have invoked the name of the village from his past that had long tormented him. His mentioning of it now was no different than any other place in the world, far removed from his study and tea. He consigned his war experiences to that of a page in a history book, which he now closed. He was captivated with a sense of elation at the prospects that lie ahead. Pavel realized that he had now left the war for good.

"The good, the bad, and the ugly of it all, Donbas is my home," thought Pavel. "The roots of my family history strike deep in this, my native soil."

Taking in the moment, Pavel found that he was happier than he had ever been before. It was the simple life of just enjoying the blessings of family and friends. It was the life he never knew he really wanted.

"I have an announcement to make," said Savka, as she clanged a glass. Wade looked at her with a nervous expression.

"If it's a boy, we'll name him Vasyli."

"Hurrah!" cheered the crowd in unison.

Wade held Savka in his arms. "The world only gets one Steve Perry and only one Savka Koval," he joked, pressing her to him for another kiss.

"Wade, what are your plans?" asked Anton.

"Well, a couple weeks ago I almost died, and now I'm eligible for Ukrainian citizenship, so I think I'll stay."

"Here in Zolote?" asked Anton, in shock.

"For now. But I've always liked the Carpathian region. I was hoping to settle down there and be a farmer. I need a place to raise my pet goose," he said with an American cowboy smile.

Четыре

An hour after his last guest had left, the newlyweds were on the road to Odessa, where they would spend a week. Pavel and Yelizaveta had their hands full watching little Anna. After he and his wife got their granddaughter to fall asleep, Pavel decided to take on the task of cleaning out of his father's old room. Walking in, he took in the intoxicating scent of linseed oil. Then he sat on the bed and glanced at the familiar array of his father's paintings. Four of them hung on the wall, all pastoral landscapes. Pavel enjoyed how the vibrant blues and gray-toned hues of the sky contrasted with the free-flowing horizontal composition of earthen tones of the fields and towns beneath. From left to right, he discovered the way each captured the quintessence of the four successive seasons. Seeing it left him with a settled tranquility, as if he and his father had a shared moment. Upon closer inspection, he recognized the vantage points. They were of various scenes from the town of Zolote. Yet, conspicuously absent was any trace of the war.

In the corner, near the window, he spied a cloth-draped easel. After walking over to inspect, he pulled the tablecloth back, revealing a portrait. It was of his mother. In hues of rich cerulean, his father had captured her kind eyes. His father's palette rested on the easel; its vibrant colors were themselves a kind of painting.

Resting at the easel's base was a fresh canvas. "Is there anything as beautiful as a blank canvas?" he thought.

Wondering if he would ever have time for oil painting, he decided then and there to make time.

"This will be my studio," he thought. "That is, if the idea holds with the ladies of the house."

Standing up to investigate the room's contents, he made another discovery. Under his father's bed was a box that contained a ham radio. It was complete with headset and microphone. Then, it all dawned on him in a torrent of recovery. Mirth rose in Pavel's throat, exploding in a wild laugh. "How could I have been so slow? It's the broadcasting studio of Tryzub 101.7 FM," he murmured.

Putting the radio back in the box, he slid it back under the bed. "I'll have you up and running in no time," he thought.

Pavel left the room and closed the door. He would be back. He soon found himself sitting in his old high-back chair and became lost again in thought.

"When Wade returns," he thought, "I'll invite him to be my apprentice in the butcher shop. After all, nepotism is an important part of our culture."

Settling down softly in his chair, Pavel sensed he had, at last, found some meaning in his life. Yet, his story, like everyone else's, remained one seeking a conclusion. Oh, what he wouldn't do to have his father see him now.

"Afganets. What are you doing?" asked Stepan.

"Just enjoying a quiet moment to myself, but I'm glad you're here my friend. What good is having something pleasurable, if you don't have a friend to share it with?" he said, pouring Stepan a glass of vodka.

"What are you thinking about?" asked Stepan.

"I was just thinking there's a potential Vadim Baranov in us all. That is, one that's capable of sacrificing others on the altar of expedience."

"I thought you'd rather be musing about the progress of this current war," said Stepan.

"Well, I might suggest a different strategy for our government to use," said Pavel, "but then again, the cobbler who criticized the work of the great court pianist, was listened to with respect, so long as he confined his observations within the limits of his own practical knowledge. In short, we can't blame everything on the government!"

"Pavel, I do believe you are becoming the patron saint of rational inquiry," said Stepan.

"Why, thank you, my friend! I do believe you'll make a Stoic out of me yet!"

"So," added Stepan, "one might venture to say, only time will tell if our situation here will go on like this, to eventually become like North and South Korea, or whether the Russians will in fact complete their invasion."

"Something like that, I suppose," mused Pavel, raising his glass, "The fight for the soul of Ukraine will go on. Za zda-ró-vye!"

"Za zda-ró-vye!" echoed Stepan. "As you say, only time will tell."

Acknowledgements

In writing this novel, I have been overwhelmed by the generous scale of help that I have received. I especially thank my daughter Collette, and my sister Maryanne Phelps. They both read the draft and provided me with invaluable insights and feedback. God bless you both!

Books by Blacksmith Publishing

Small Unit Tactics Handbook

Fire in the Jungle

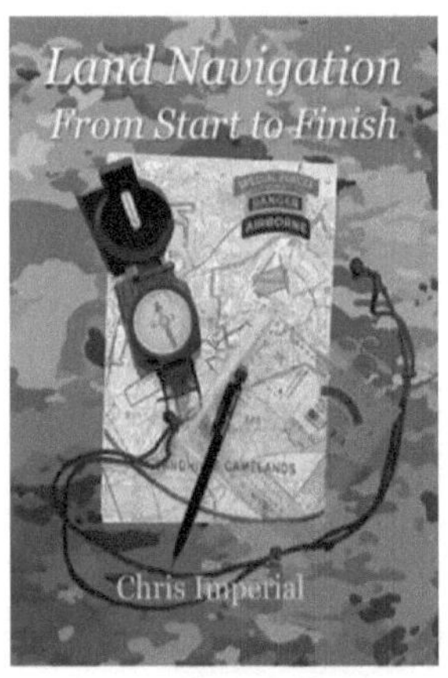

Land Navigation From Start to Finish

Tactical Leadership

www.blacksmithpublishingcom